Not the ideal summer vacation

"So, let me get this straight. I'm supposed to go stay with people who, technically, are *family*, but I've never actually met?"

He nodded.

"And what exactly am I supposed to do there for six whole weeks?"

He gave me a small, tentative smile, as if to say there's hope for this kid yet. "Your great-uncle is heading a project that involves math—a lot of math. It will be of great value to you. He's building an artesian screw." Dad immediately screwed up his face, maybe to look artesian. . . . "I said that you would assist with this artesian screw project."

Great. I was artesianly screwed.

"Do you want to know the best part of this whole experience for you? I believe it might help you get into Newton."

Was he serious? Newton High? A math magnet school? I'm no statistician, but what are the odds of a kid with dyscalculia—*a math learning disability!*—getting into a math magnet school? Oh, yeah . . . Newton High was a feeder school for his university, and Dad did a lot for Newton. They'd probably accept a token math moron just to thank him.

OTHER BOOKS YOU MAY ENJOY

the absolute VALUE of MIKE

Kathryn Erskine

PUFFIN BOOKS
An Imprint of Penguin Group (USA) Inc.

PUFFIN BOOKS
Published by the Penguin Group
Penguin Young Readers Group, 345 Hudson Street, New York, New York 10014, U.S.A.
Penguin Group (Canada), 90 Eglinton Avenue East, Suite 700, Toronto, Ontario, Canada M4P 2Y3
(a division of Pearson Penguin Canada Inc.)
Penguin Books Ltd, 80 Strand, London WC2R 0RL, England
Penguin Ireland, 25 St Stephen's Green, Dublin 2, Ireland (a division of Penguin Books Ltd)
Penguin Group (Australia), 250 Camberwell Road, Camberwell, Victoria 3124, Australia
(a division of Pearson Australia Group Pty Ltd)
Penguin Books India Pvt Ltd, 11 Community Centre,
Panchsheel Park, New Delhi - 110 017, India
Penguin Group (NZ), 67 Apollo Drive, Rosedale, Auckland 0632, New Zealand
(a division of Pearson New Zealand Ltd.)
Penguin Books (South Africa) (Pty) Ltd, 24 Sturdee Avenue,
Rosebank, Johannesburg 2196, South Africa

Registered Offices: Penguin Books Ltd, 80 Strand, London WC2R 0RL, England

First published in the United States of America by Philomel Books,
a division of Penguin Young Readers Group, 2011
Published by Puffin Books, a division of Penguin Young Readers Group, 2012

3 5 7 9 10 8 6 4

THE LIBRARY OF CONGRESS HAS CATALOGED THE PHILOMEL BOOKS EDITION AS FOLLOWS:
Erskine, Kathryn.
The absolute value of Mike / Kathryn Erskine.
p. cm.
Summary: Fourteen-year-old Mike, whose father is a brilliant mathematician
but who has no math aptitude himself, spends the summer in rural
Pennsylvania with his elderly and eccentric relatives Moo and Poppy,
helping the townspeople raise money to adopt a Romanian orphan.
ISBN: 978-0-399-25505-2 (hc)
[1. Fathers and sons—Fiction. 2. Self-acceptance—Fiction.
3. Individuality—Fiction. 4. Eccentrics and eccentricities—Fiction.
5. Business enterprises—Fiction. 6. Pennsylvania—Fiction.]
I. Title.
PZ7.E7388Ab 2011
[Fic]—dc22   2010013333

Puffin Books ISBN 978-0-14-242101-7

Edited by Tamra Tuller. Design by Semadar Megged.
Set in Trump Mediaevel

Printed in the United States of America

ALWAYS LEARNING   PEARSON

To Gavin, whose strength of mind and spirit

has taught me much about the

absolute value of life

the
ABSOLUTE
VALUE
of
MIKE

1

PARALLEL LINES

—lines in the same plane that do not intersect

y cell phone rang just as I was about to crush the Emperor of Doom's trebuchet and save the villagers from certain annihilation.

It was the ominous beats of Beethoven's Symphony no. 5. Da-da-da-daaaa. "Yes, Dad, what is it?"

"Could you come here, please?"

Why didn't he shout my name like a normal parent?

I walked next door to the study and flicked the light switch on. He was pushing piles of schematic diagrams around his desk, sending dozens of small Snickers wrappers onto the floor. Dinner. I picked them up, along with the chunks of chocolate that fell on the rug, and shook my head. Dad was probably fifty pounds heavier than he should be—the Giant Genius.

"Dad, when Dr. McGovern said to reduce your fat intake, I don't think he meant reduce the size of your candy bars. I bet he was thinking more like . . . salad."

"I don't eat salad." Dad's voice didn't match his frantic fingers flipping through the piles on his desk.

"What are you looking for, anyway?"

No answer. His gray head was stooped so low that the glasses he'd shoved on top of it were staring straight at me.

Glasses. "Have you checked your head recently?" I asked.

He blinked up at me, then up at his forehead. "Ah. It's actually my keys I seem to have misplaced." But I noticed he put his glasses on anyway.

"Did you try your pocket?"

He patted his left pants pocket and I heard the familiar jangle. "Ahhh. Thank you." He stood up and grabbed his jacket off of the computer monitor. "Must run. Teaching tonight. Seminar this summer, Romania."

Dad had been teaching Math for Electrical Engineers for so long, he spoke in isolated packets of energy, like he'd turned into electricity himself. I pinched my nose to do my robot voice. "Too much resistance. Please complete circuit. Thank you."

Dad took a deep breath. "I will be in Romania for six weeks this summer, lecturing at the university there and working on my book."

Romania? The first thing I thought was, *Hey, isn't that near Russia, where Sasha was adopted from?* Then the full effect of what Dad said hit me like an electrical charge. I stared at him. "Romania? You can't go away—I mean, by yourself. How are you going to survive? Dude, you can't even find your car keys without me!"

He blinked up at the ceiling. "Car keys won't be necessary. I won't be driving."

I won't be driving? Is that all he could say? "But—how about all the regular, everyday stuff?" He couldn't do anything for himself—pay bills, make toast, find shoes that match.

He stared at me for a second, which is about as long as he can hold a stare. "Room and board is provided."

"Fine," I sputtered. "I'll take care of everything here." As usual. I crushed the Snickers wrappers in my fist.

Dad cleared his throat. "My colleagues inform me that it's inappropriate to leave a, uh"—he squinted at the ceiling—"a . . . thirteen-year-old home alone."

"Fourteen, Dad." *Do the math. You're the genius.*

"Ah. Nevertheless, I believe the minimum age stated was sixteen."

Wait a minute . . . if I couldn't stay by myself . . . that meant he was taking me with him! "Dad! We're going to Romania? A trip? Just like Sasha and his parents? Sweeeet! Why didn't you say—"

"No unsupervised minors allowed."

I felt the chunks of chocolate melting in my hand. "I—I can take care of myself." Shoot, I'd been taking care of myself—and him—for years.

Dad shook his head. "Obviously, I will not be able to supervise you there."

I dropped the Snickers wrappers. "Dad. You don't supervise me here, either." Hadn't he ever noticed that?

He paused and I thought I had him, but all he did was put on his jacket. "I've contacted the aunt and uncle whom I visited in rural Pennsylvania every summer as a boy. You'll be staying with them."

Rural Pennsylvania? Wasn't that where the groundhog lived? And if he saw his shadow, it was six more weeks of doom? This was even worse than Sasha's upcoming vacation. Wait a minute! Sasha!

"Hey, Dad, if you're going to send me away somewhere, can't I go backpacking with Sasha's family? They've always said I could go with them whenever I want." And, boy, did I want. The Canadian Rockies for the entire summer with no cell phones, iPods, or laptops—much as Sasha and I had cursed up and down about it—sounded like nirvana compared to Groundhogsville with some old relatives I'd never met.

Dad pushed his fingertips together and flexed his fingers, gazing at them like he'd created some engineering puzzle. "Sasha's father informed me it was a family bonding trip."

Mr. Namboodri had only said that to give Dad a clue that maybe our family could use a little bonding. Of course, Dad didn't pick up on the hint.

"I'm practically like family to them."

Dad shook his head. "And your school . . . touchy-feely person—"

"Counselor, Dad. Mr. McMillin." I still wonder what Dad wrote on my third-quarter report card to make Mr. McMillin call us in for that awkward "little chat." He kept giving me sad-puppy looks while he emphasized the word *family* to Dad, saying that I was at the age where I needed to know how much my *family* cared about me.

And that, being a boy, I needed a male role model from my *family*. He was trying not to be too obvious so as not to embarrass Dad. The truth is, you have to be really direct with Dad or he doesn't get it. Like sending me to live with complete strangers.

I stared at Dad. "So, let me get this straight. I'm supposed to go stay with people who, technically, are *family*, but I've never actually met?"

He nodded.

"And what exactly am I supposed to do there for six whole weeks?"

He gave me a small, tentative smile, as if to say there's hope for this kid yet. "Your great-uncle is heading a project that involves math—a lot of math. It will be of great value to you. He's building an artesian screw." Dad immediately screwed up his face, maybe to look artesian. "I don't understand the logic of that because, obviously, a water screw is designed to force water to rise, but artesian water rises naturally." He shook his head. "Still, I said that you would assist with this artesian screw project."

Great. I was artesianly screwed.

"I believe this project will help you with your math skills. You'll learn about oblique angles—those are acute or obtuse angles—and intervals—those are arrangements of elements of a set—as well as properties of physics!"

This was Dad at his most excited. Math. Science. Engineering.

I tried to look interested. I tried to look like I cared. Okay, I tried not to yawn.

"You may be building a water turbine—that's a device

that takes the kinetic energy of a moving fluid, converting it into mechanical power and—" He stopped himself and smiled at me. "Do you want to know the best part of this whole experience for you? I believe it might help you get into Newton."

Was he serious? Newton High? A math magnet school? I'm no statistician, but what are the odds of a kid with dyscalculia—*a math learning disability!*—getting into a math magnet school? Oh, yeah . . . Newton High was a feeder school for his university, and Dad did a lot for Newton. They'd probably accept a token math moron just to thank him.

"Dad, really, there's nothing wrong with the regular high school."

"You need to stand out in order to be accepted at a good university. Therefore, Newton High is the only choice." He sighed and picked up the photo from his desk. It was of Mom and me with the huge LEGO drawbridge I made for Dad's birthday when I was six. "Your mother always said you'd be a great engineer." His voice was quiet. As if he were talking to Mom, not me. Like he was asking her what went wrong. And how it was possible that he'd ended up with me, Michael Einstein Frost, ignorant spawn of the genius James Elliot Frost, P-H-D.

I slumped back against Dad's bookshelf and felt the blue LEGO brick that was always in my pocket. Mom called me her "little engineer" when I made LEGO creations with my friends at Montessori or when I got all the kids on the beach to help me make the biggest sand castle, but it was when I made that drawbridge—it actually worked!—and Dad laughed and hugged me that she called me a *"great engineer."* Come to think of it, that's the last time I remember Dad laughing or hugging me. Soon after that, Mom was gone.

"I think you'd learn a great deal from this project," Dad said, still staring at the photo. "I'd like to see you master math or engineering at an acceptable level, at least. If you can't solve the simplest problems—"

"I know, Dad. I'll end up on the street." How many times had I heard that?

That's when my toes started wiggling and I knew I was about to have a brilliant idea. It always starts in my feet, and by the time I realize my toes are moving, the idea makes it up to my brain. And there it was.

If I could ace this artesian screw, maybe Dad would be satisfied that I'd "mastered math or engineering at an acceptable level." Then, I could show him how I could take care of myself and not end up on the street. And maybe he'd let me just go to a regular high school. Someday he'd have to accept the fact that I could never be a math genius, much as he tried to teach me and have me tutored and send me to special camps. He still had hope for me. For some reason, I just didn't have the heart to make him see the truth.

The plan had to work. The alternative, going to Newton High, where I'd flunk out for sure, meant a miserable me and a seriously disappointed Dad. As far as I could see, there were two hurdles: (1) ace the project and (2) get my great-uncle to convince Dad that I was a great engineer. The first hurdle was up to me, and I had a lot of practice at pretending I understood math when I really didn't. The second was an unknown.

"Hey, Dad? What's your uncle like?"

Dad chewed his lip and looked away. Of course. It wasn't the kind of question Dad could answer. It was about people. "I don't know where he received his engineering education and I'm not aware of all of his qualifications. Oh, and, uh . . . Mike?" He looked at me in that cloudy way he had.

Why did he always have to stop and think before saying my name?

"What?"

"You'll need to remember that these relatives are now oc-to-ge-nar-i-ans." He carefully pronounced every syllable since, ob-vi-ous-ly, I'm stupid.

"Meaning . . . they're eight-armed mutants?" I knew what *octogenarian* meant, but I wanted to see if I could get him.

"It means they're in their eighties," he said slowly. "They are elderly."

I nodded seriously. "Gotcha."

"They may have difficulty hearing you or understanding you."

So instead of Dad not understanding me, I'd have . . . "What are their names?"

Dad blew at a spot on the monitor and wiped it. "Uh . . . Poppy and Moo."

"*Poppy and Moo*? Are you kidding me? Dad! You're sending me to live with farm animals?"

He sighed. "You're going to have to control your impulsive behavior, given the demise they've recently suffered." Dad's gauge for impulsive behavior was a possum. Preferably a dead one. "Their only son died a few months ago. In a car accident."

Like Mom. Jeez. The familiar dull ache hit my throat. I didn't know what to say. And then I couldn't help thinking, *What if I die in a car accident while he's over in Romania? He'll have no one.*

And he wouldn't even be able to picture my face, because he's got this weird condition where he can't make a mental image of a face, even of someone he's lived with for fourteen years. Like me.

I glanced over at his monitor and saw my reflection. Like a shadow. Of a groundhog. Six weeks of doom. I turned away quickly. "Hey, Dad—"

But I heard the front door close. He was gone.

2

TRANSVERSAL LINE

—a line that passes through two or
more other lines at different points

Moo's white hair stuck straight out, like the wings of the commuter jet I'd just flown in on. Her glasses covered most of her face. The rest of it was giving me an entire-set-of-dentures grin.

"I'm so sorry I'm late, dear, but this airport is terribly confusing. See?" She pointed at the sign above the gangway door I'd exited from my plane. "It says Exit 88. How many exits do we need?"

"Actually," I corrected her, "it says *Gate 3B*."

She squinted at it. "Oh. Well, that's a bad sign." She held out her tiny pale hand. "Anyway, I'm glad to finally meet you, dear. Do you like scrapple?"

I stared at her. "Excuse me?"

She took a step closer and looked up at me. Even though I wasn't that tall, I still towered over her. "Scrapple," she repeated.

What the heck was scrapple? "What?"

She chewed her lip for a moment and waved her hand at me, and I bent my head down to her level.

I could hear her taking a big, raspy breath. "SCRAPPLE," she shouted.

"Ow!" I put my hand over my ringing ear.

"Oh, that must be your good ear. My left ear is my good one, too! We already have something in common." She patted my hand—the one that wasn't holding my ear. "We need to go to Shop 'n Save because I want to buy you some food and Poppy really needs his scrapple."

I stared at her stupidly because I couldn't think of what to say.

Moo gazed at me, her smeared red lipstick making her smile even broader. "You look like your father, dear. Only not as . . ."

Smart. "Yeah, I know."

She glanced at the Exit 88/Gate 3B sign for a moment, then looked around the concourse as if she were lost. "But I can't see you."

"I'M RIGHT HERE."

She flinched and turned her owl glasses to me. "I know, dear. What I meant was I can't see your eyes because your hair is in front of them."

I tried pushing some hair out of my eyes, but it didn't work very well. My hair grows in stupid swirls all over the place. I figure it's a commentary on what's directly underneath.

"Your hair is very different from your father's. James's hair was so limp. Yours is—well, you just don't see that many people with cowlicks."

"That's because I got all of theirs."

"Would you like me to give you a trim?" She reached over and touched one of my swirls.

I cringed at the thought of someone with her eyesight cutting my hair.

"Oh, that's right, James hated anyone touching his hair, too." She sighed. "At least you don't cover your ears and scream."

"Excuse me? Dad used to do that?"

"Yes. You mean he's outgrown that?"

"Yeah, well . . . he's fifty-six now. What else did he used to do?"

"Well, he was always forgetting things."

"He still does."

"And he loved candy."

"That hasn't changed, either."

"He had . . . unusual ideas."

"That's because he's a genius."

"Oh, is that what they're calling it now?"

"What?"

"Never mind. I'm glad to hear he's grown up a little. It takes some of us a long time, doesn't it? Still, little steps eventually get us somewhere. Speaking of which, we need to get moving." She turned and started off the way she came, her pale yellow sneakers looking like duck feet padding down the concourse, pushing through the small crowd of people.

I grabbed my backpack and sports bag and followed her.

"James said you're going to help Poppy, and I must say,

he could certainly use the help. Are you good at working with wood?"

I thought about my C's in shop class. It was the fine corners I wasn't any good at. But a screw didn't have fine corners. "Woodworking? I can't get enough of it!"

She clapped her hands. "That's wonderful, Mike!"

"What exactly am I going to be doing?"

"Oh, Poppy will let you know." Her smile remained frozen. "Eventually."

"Eventually?"

But she hurried on. "I want you to have some fun, too! All work and no play makes James a very dull boy."

"I think it's 'makes *Jack* a very dull boy.' James is my dad."

She smiled broadly and touched her forefinger to her chin. "I know, dear."

Wait—was she calling Dad dull? But I couldn't stop to think. I practically had to jog to keep up with her. Tiny as she was, that lady could move.

"Your dad sent some scrap paper for you. I'm glad to see he recycles old school papers. It has all kinds of numbers and symbols and nonsense on the back, but he said you could use it."

As forgetful as Dad was, he hadn't forgotten summer math worksheets. The numbers and symbols made about as much sense to me as they did to Moo. I definitely needed to concentrate on the artesian screw. It'd be the perfect excuse for why I didn't get to the stack of worksheets.

"Is it for ara—, agar—, goomee . . . what's that folding paper thing?"

"Origami?"

"That's it! Is that what you do with all that paper?"

"Pretty much." If that's what you called crumpling it into balls, throwing it at the wall, and jumping up and down on it while cursing.

"Well, I'm sure you'll do something very special with it. Come along, now!" She readjusted her red purse that was so large it would have to be considered checked luggage, and I watched it bang against the back of her white hoodie as she walked down the concourse. The picture of the white-haired woman on the cover of my old Mother Goose book flashed across my mind.

I caught up with her and she grabbed my arm, maybe worried that I'd fall behind again. "Tell me, what do you like to do for fun?"

Fun? I hadn't thought of that possibility. "Do you guys have a PlayStation or Xbox or anything like that?"

"Oh, play station! Yes, it's in the attic because we haven't used it since Doug—" She let go of me and stopped, grabbing the strings of her hoodie and yanking so hard, I thought she might strangle herself. She sucked her lips and I didn't see any evidence of breathing. I was about to slap her on the back to make her snap out of it when she suddenly opened her mouth and gasped.

"Play station," she repeated, with a definitive nod but watery eyes, like she'd just recovered from a painful blow but was standing back up in the ring again. "Yes. Most of the little people are gone, but the cars are still there, along with the gas pump. The plastic hose from the gas pump is a little chewed up, but it still fits into the cars."

She smiled up at me and I read the big red letters on the front of her hoodie that shouted HOLY COMFORTER, even though the voice inside my head was shouting, *Holy crap!*

"Please tell me you have a computer." Dad made me leave my cell phone at home so I wouldn't be "distracted from the mission." I had a cheap MP3 player but absolutely no link to the outside world.

"No computer, but they have some nice new ones at the bank. In color! Gladys loves to show off her new computer. She even gave it a name. She calls it 'Mac.' Isn't that cute?"

I looked away so she wouldn't see my face and stared into Bound for Adventure Books and Videos as we walked past. Of course. Movies. "Do you have any DVDs?"

She stopped and clutched my arm again, blinking up at me. "Oh, dear. You didn't bring any of yours?"

"No. Don't you guys have any?"

"Well, Poppy has some, of course. But they wouldn't do for you. Not at all. We'll buy you some, though. What size BVDs do you need?"

"Size? What do you mean?"

She took a deep, raspy breath. "UNDERPANTS, dear. What SIZE BEE-VEE-DEES do you wear?"

The wave of travelers seemed to settle around Moo's duck feet, gaping at me.

"I—I said DEE-VEE-DEE! You know, like a video? A movie?"

"Oh, that's what you're talking about!"

There's not a whole lot more embarrassing than having your great-aunt shout about your underwear in the middle of an airport. I felt like everyone was staring at where my boxers were. I rushed ahead through the automatic doors to get outside.

"Wait for me, dear!" I heard Moo call after me. "You don't even know where I left Tyrone!"

I turned around and watched her come through the doors behind me. "Tyrone?"

"Yes, dear. How do you expect to find him without me?"

"Who's . . . is that Poppy?"

"Goodness, no! Poppy and Tyrone don't get along at all." She grinned. "Poppy thinks I spend entirely too much time and money on Tyrone. I think he's a little jealous."

I had this momentary frightening image of a little old lady having an affair with a boy toy. I shook my head hard to get rid of it. "So . . . who's Tyrone?" I wasn't entirely sure I wanted to know.

3

SKEW LINES

—lines that do not intersect
but are not parallel and exist
only in three dimensions

A car? Tyrone is a car?"

"Yes, he's a Ford Tor—, Tar—"

"Taurus."

"See? Who can remember a silly name like that? I like Tyrone much better. It's a lovely name, don't you think?"

I decided to play along and opened the door of the backseat. "I'll just put my bags in Tyrone's back pocket—" I stopped when I saw what was inside. The backseat was covered in red velvet, including the armrest. There were movie posters on the backs of the front seats, the door panels, and the roof of the car. *Gone with the Wind. The Sound of Music. The Wizard of Oz.* Even *Under Siege, Die Hard*, and *The Terminator*.

I stared. And sniffed. "It smells like popcorn."

"It must be left over from Sunday's matinee."

"Excuse me?"

"Sunday afternoons I come in here and watch movies."

"How?"

"Oh, my dear, I know those old movies so well, I just look at the poster and it all comes back to me. It's much cheaper than going out to a regular theater."

I threw my bags in the "theater" and sat next to Moo.

She dropped her huge purse in my lap. The thing must've weighed fifteen pounds. "You take care of Junior."

"Junior?"

"Yes, I've downsized drastically." She put both hands on top of the steering wheel, which was covered with bright orange fuzzy fabric.

"What was it before? A U-Haul?"

But I didn't hear her answer because Tyrone shot out of the parking space faster than the Emperor of Doom's trebuchet could fling a cannonball.

"Whoa!" I grabbed on to the dashboard.

"Tyrone has a mind of his own, dear, but he's an excellent driver."

The way she put her hands up on the wheel made it look like she was trying to climb a ladder so she could see what was over the top . . . of the dashboard. I wasn't old enough to drive, but it seemed to me you should be looking above the steering wheel, not through it.

"Moo? Can you see okay?"

"Of course I can!" she snapped. "There's nothing wrong with my eyes. Now, help me read the signs."

Talk about the blind leading the blind. We circled the

parking garage three times before I persuaded her to take the ramp with the Exit sign above it. She thought the sign said Erie and asked, "We don't want to go all the way up there, do we?"

I wasn't sure we'd even get all the way to her house, what with the gurgling, knocking noises coming out of Tyrone. After several minutes Moo started coughing along with him.

"What's that noise?"

Moo sniffed. "Allergies."

"No, I meant Tyrone."

"So did I. They're seasonal, though. He does much better in the fall."

Tyrone's allergies didn't seem to slow him down at all. I kept my eyes peeled in case Moo couldn't see something that I could. Like other cars. And the road. I wouldn't say I was an extra set of eyes exactly. More like the only set of eyes.

Moo kept looking over at me and smiling. I thought if I stared out the windshield she might follow my example. It didn't work. Instead, she stared at me and said, "We're all lost, aren't we, dear?"

"I—I don't think so. We're headed for your house, right?"

"I mean your shirt."

I looked down. It was my Doves T-shirt, from their *Lost Souls* album.

"Don't worry. I'm a collector of lost souls." I didn't have a chance to wonder what she meant. Before I knew it, Moo was veering off onto the grassy median. I lurched in my seat and grabbed the wheel, jerking Tyrone back onto the highway.

Moo pointed to the road ahead. "That's our town!"

I looked at the sign as we exited. *"Do Over*? That's the name of your town?"

"It's Donover, but the *n* went missing a long time ago."

"Why doesn't someone fix it?"

"Oh, I don't know. I rather like 'Do Over,' don't you?"

"It sounds like something was wrong the first time."

"Well, maybe there was. Do Over is a second chance. Sometimes we need a second chance."

Moo nodded at an abandoned Exxon station. "That's where the flea market is on Thursdays and Saturdays. And that's where . . ." Her voice trailed off as she looked to her left at Big Dawg's Tattoo and Bar. "You don't need to know about that place."

I saw an orange warning sign for road construction. "Slow down!"

"I told you, dear, Tyrone has a mind of his own."

I hit the dashboard a couple of times. "Tyrone! Dude! Slow down!"

Moo peered over the steering wheel at the roadwork. "I think the orange team needs to find a better place for their soccer game, don't you, Mike?"

"They're construction workers! They're wearing orange vests so you can *see* them."

"Oh. Well, goodness, they don't have to dart all over the road like squirrels." She looked over at me, dragging the wheel to the right, narrowly missing a guy in a yellow hard hat. "It's just not safe."

Tyrone crunched over several traffic cones before lurching to an almost complete stop and turning without using a signal. Horns blared behind us. Moo explained that Tyrone's "ticky-ticky" wasn't working, by which I figured out she meant the turn signal.

"How does anyone know when you're turning?"

"Well, *I* know when I'm turning, Mike. That's what counts. Goodness, other people are busy with their own lives. They can't worry about where I'm going."

"Uh, actually, they do, because—" But I stopped as Tyrone made some particularly weird sputtering noises and lurched to a stop in front of a Kmart.

I looked at Moo. "What's wrong? Allergies?"

"I'm afraid Tyrone's out of gas, but we can walk home from here. It's not that far."

But it was as hot as a furnace. "Can't Poppy pick us up?"

"He's . . . busy." Moo took the keys out of the ignition and put them in Junior. "Oh, dear, we didn't get to buy scrapple for—"

The blare of an air horn drowned out anything else she was saying and made me jump and reel around to look out of the rear window. An eighteen-wheeler practically sliced off Tyrone's butt, which was kind of stuck out in the lane because of Moo's parking job.

". . . and we need to be careful of the trucks, dear."

"No kidding! Get out of the car, fast, before the next one comes!"

She smiled back. "It's rather a nice day for a walk, isn't it, Mike?"

With the semis?

I grabbed my bags out of Tyrone's theater and followed Moo down the rural highway. A semi blasted its horn over and over and I thought it was going to run us down, but Moo was laughing, her fist pumping up and down like she was pulling a chain.

Five more semis went blasting past, Moo pumping her fist at each one. I was panting like a dog from the sun, my bags, and the horns, but I literally jumped when a horn blared right behind us, a whole string of notes that sounded out "Dixie."

A black Ford F-350 swerved right by us, missing us by inches, and honked again. The driver's long hair was flying wildly around his face, but I could see that he was laughing.

"What the—"

"NUMNUT!" Moo screamed.

"No kidding!" I watched the pickup, loaded with drums and amps bouncing in the back, as it raced away from us.

"Gladys's boyfriend."

"What?"

"GLADYS," Moo shouted, "from the bank."

"He's an idiot!"

"Yes, he is. We're all waiting for Gladys to dump him. Again."

"She sounds a little clueless."

"Oh, she's very bright, Mike, super smart. But not when it comes to men, I'm afraid."

"Obviously."

I wondered if Gladys was one of Moo's "lost souls."

A few minutes later, we finally turned off of the main road and passed a couple of houses before Moo walked up a gravel driveway. A white Chevy Suburban with a dented bumper sat at the end of the driveway, in front of an old garage. I followed Moo, walking past their mailbox, which had a Harley-Davidson motorcycle carved on top.

It was an ordinary small white frame house except for the fact that the front porch and steps were carpeted. In an orange and red swirly pattern. Even weirder was the array of colorful plastic buckets and bowls sitting upright in the yard.

"I bet I know exactly what you're thinking," Moo said from the top step.

I was thinking a lot of things. Like, *What's up with the buckets?* And, *Am I really stuck here for six weeks?* Even, *If this is some bizarre video game, how do I quit?*

Moo nodded knowingly. "You're thinking, West Nile virus. But don't you worry, I never let any water sit in those buckets, so no mosquitoes can breed West Nile virus. And I put a little vinegar in each bucket because bugs hate vinegar. As soon as the rain stops, I empty all the tubs into my big covered trash can in the vegetable garden out back to use for watering later. Water isn't cheap, you know."

Moo held the front door open for me and I caught a whiff of mothballs. I recognized the smell from our attic, where Dad kept the bags of Mom's clothes. I asked him why he didn't give them to the Namboodris' church to send to orphans and homeless people in eastern Europe. All Dad did was stare into the distance and mumble something about mothballs preserving things.

"Come on in, dear!"

Moo disappeared inside. "Poppy! Mike's here, and do you know what? He got me home from the airport. Isn't that amazing? Mike, come meet Poppy!"

As I tried to adjust my eyes to the darkness, I noticed the walls were covered in portraits. It was a good thing Dad wasn't there. He'd be freaked by this many sets of eyes staring at him. "Who are all these people?"

"They're portraits nobody wanted. I call them 'instant ancestors.' I'm a regular URL—Unwanteds Rescue League." She grinned at me. "I take care of all the rejects."

Rejects? Like me? I wiped the sweat from my upper lip and told myself she was just an old lady, and a pretty wacky one at that. She really wasn't calling me a reject. Not on purpose, anyway. Still, I was getting hotter. And sweaty. And dizzy. Then I realized what was wrong. It was about a hundred degrees in the house. It was amazing the paintings weren't melting.

"Moo?" My voice was dry, cracking, weak. "Where's the thermostat?"

"What, dear?"

I cleared my throat. "We need to turn the AC on."

"The what?"

"The AC," I said, louder, remembering her bad ear. "AIR-conditioning."

"We just have fans, dear."

"Can we turn them on?"

She chewed her lip. "You must be hot, Mike. Are you feeling all right?"

Me? I looked at her and realized that she was still wearing her HOLY COMFORTER hoodie. "Aren't you hot?"

"Not really, dear."

"What about . . . Poppy?"

"I don't think he feels the heat."

Where was Poppy, anyway? Behind the living room was the kitchen. I could tell because of a doorway and a pass-through cut in the wall. Beside the doorway and pass-through was a TV. Opposite the TV, a white couch with an orange afghan sat under the front window. In front of the couch was a coffee table that had a bunch of Oprah magazines with a bright yellow yardstick on top of them. I followed the line of the yardstick, which seemed to point to a huge recliner in the far, dark corner of the room. With a statue sitting in it.

At least, it was frozen like a statue. Its arms were almost as white as its undershirt except for the blue veins running up and down. Above the undershirt, hair peeked out, then a fat neck and stubbly chin. Lips stuck out in a pout. Eyes stared straight ahead. Two tufts of gray hair stuck up like devil horns. The whole statue looked like it hadn't moved in days.

"Say hello to Poppy!" Moo said.

4

PLACE VALUE

—place value identifies the
value of each digit

Poppy didn't move. Even when a fly landed on his hand. I was sure he was dead. How long had he been dead? Is that why she had mothballs? Was Moo preserving him?

"He's very quiet," said Moo.

"Y-Yeah. Real quiet. How—how long has he been this quiet?"

She whispered in my good ear. "Since the death—"

"Oh, jeez!" He was dead!

"I'm sorry, Mike, didn't your dad tell you?" She pulled on her hoodie strings. "Doug died four months ago and Poppy just hasn't been able to deal with it."

"Oh! You mean your son."

Moo pulled harder on the strings of her HOLY COMFORTER hoodie. I gently pulled on the back of her hood to give it some slack. Her little fists rose with the strings as I pulled. Eventually she let go and rubbed her arms and shoulders like she was cold.

"Sorry about Doug," I mumbled. I looked over at the wax figure. "But Poppy's . . . uh . . . still with us?"

She tapped the side of her head with her finger. "He's away with the fairies."

"Huh?"

"He just sits there and thinks about Doug. He won't do anything else, won't talk to anyone. Not even me. Just looks at the TEE-Vee. And eats scrapple."

The TV was off. Poppy hadn't moved. The fly was still on his arm. "When exactly was the last time he ate scrapple?"

"Breakfast this morning. He never eats lunch and hardly touches dinner. But I always fix him scrapple for breakfast because he can really put that stuff away. I think it's the only thing that keeps him alive."

I finally exhaled fully. At least he wasn't dead. But he wasn't exactly lively, either. And then it hit me. Holy crap! "Moo? What about the artesian screw?"

Moo sighed and shook her head, plodding into the kitchen with Junior.

What did that mean? I followed her, my backpack banging against the wall phone to my left and knocking the receiver off. I put the receiver back in its cradle after untangling the old cord that was duct-taped together in three places. I thought about calling Dad. He'd said to call only in a "dire emergency." Since Poppy wasn't actually a corpse, there was no dire emergency. And I sure didn't want to admit that the artesian screw might be a bust. He'd just send more math problems. And he'd be more determined than ever to send me to the math and science school. Which meant more failure. More disappointment.

"So, Moo, where's the artesian screw, anyway?"

Moo shook her head and whispered, "Poppy and his helpers haven't even started."

"Oh, great." I dropped my bags on the floor. "I'm only here for six weeks, you know."

"I know."

"Is that going to be enough time?"

"I certainly hope so, dear. This is very important."

"No kidding." I glared at Poppy through the pass-through. He hadn't moved, as far as I could tell, but the yellow yardstick was now on his lap.

"Mike, why don't you try talking to Poppy? Maybe he'll listen to you."

"Me?"

She nodded, her big owl eyes looking sad yet hopeful.

I walked slowly into the living room and made myself look at the creepy figure with hair horns. "So . . . dude . . . how about that artesian screw?"

Poppy's eyes narrowed and he turned away from me to look at the cat clock on the wall. I'd seen one like it on eBay. Although it was early afternoon, the clock was stuck on ten minutes after eight and was as motionless as Poppy.

"Your clock's broken," I said.

Poppy's jaw clenched and his head dropped so far that his devil-horn tufts of hair stuck straight forward.

Moo's voice came from the kitchen. "Felix is fine. He just needs new batteries."

"Felix?"

"Felix the Cat was a cartoon character Doug loved. He used to drive Poppy crazy singing that theme song."

"Do you have any batteries? I'll put them in."

Moo beckoned to me through the pass-through and I went into the kitchen. "That's sweet of you, Mike." She glanced through the pass-through and lowered her voice. "Poppy doesn't want anyone else to put the batteries in."

"Then why doesn't he do it?"

"He doesn't want anyone but Doug to put them in. You see, Doug gave Poppy that clock for Father's Day many, many years ago. It was the first present he could actually buy for Poppy. He saved up a long time for that clock."

I looked at the grinning cat, wondering if Dad would feel that way about anything I gave him. I knew how Dad would feel about no artesian screw. "Listen, Moo, is there anything I can do to get Poppy's project started?"

Moo chewed her lip and looked through the pass-through at the Poppy lump. She leaned toward me and whispered, "I'm afraid the workshop is a mess. The first step would be to pick that place up."

"Okay, let me at it."

"Poppy doesn't like anyone going into his work-shop. It's his man-cave. But maybe we should make an exception?"

She padded into the living room, stopping at the row of keys by the front door. She checked to make sure Poppy wasn't watching, snatched a key off the wall peg, and ran back into the kitchen, shoving the key into my hand.

"Side door of the garage," she hissed, and then, obviously for Poppy's benefit, said, "Oh, Mike, WHY DON'T YOU GO OUTSIDE AND SEE MY VEGETABLE GARDEN?" She gave me a big wink.

I headed for the garage. The door of the white frame building had a window in it, but it was so dark inside, I couldn't see a thing. I stuck the key in the rusted lock, and after pushing against the door a few times, it opened. The smell of wood chips and shellac hit me and I breathed in deeply. It was a good smell and took me back to shop class at school. As I stepped into the garage to find light switches, my feet almost slipped out from under me. I skidded on something, or lots of somethings. I grabbed a workbench to stay upright.

When I looked down, I saw that the floor was covered with nails. All different sized nails. Black ones, shiny ones, large ones, small ones. It was a sea of nails. As my eyes adjusted to the darkness, I saw the rest of the mess that Moo had mentioned. Saws and files and hammers were spread out on surfaces like they'd been thrown there. Chunks of wood were strewn everywhere. If the walls hadn't been standing, I would've thought a hurricane had blown through.

There were great power tools, though: Delta Unisaw, Powermatic lathe, DeWalt drill press. Man, you could make anything in here! Against the far wall I noticed he had a ton of boards, sorted by type. Maple. Walnut.

Cherry. Maybe he was trying out different woods for the artesian screw to see which one performed best. How did you make an artesian screw, anyway?

I stumbled over the nails on the floor to get to the radial arm saw and brushed off some of the sawdust. It was my favorite tool. With a radial arm saw you could take a plank of wood and make it into a simple bookshelf. That was the project I got an A on. Mr. Barron, my shop teacher, even put it on display in the school lobby. Sasha asked what my dad thought of it. "Are you kidding?" I asked him. "Dad doesn't know about this. It's too . . . *vocational.*"

I took a piece of the maple and laid it on the table just to slice the very edge off, just to see how the saw worked, just to feel the wood and the power in my hands. It was still kind of dark but the big red button was obvious. I reached up, took a deep breath, and pressed it on.

Nothing happened. I felt my shoulders slump. Then I remembered Mr. Barron saying to always unplug power tools when not in use. I felt behind the saw and found the cord, following it all the way to the wall. Where it was plugged in. Shoot! I finally found the light switches and flicked them up and down. I stood in darkness. Nothing in this place worked!

I stormed back to the kitchen. "Where's the circuit breaker?"

"What, dear?"

"The garage is completely dead!"

She held up her forefinger in front of her mouth to

quiet me down, and whispered, "Workshop, dear. Poppy doesn't like it when people say *garage*. We don't want to upset Poppy."

I didn't care if Poppy was upset or not. "I need to turn the electricity back on."

"Oh," she said. "That. I—I didn't pay the electric bill." She pulled her hoodie strings and sniffled like she was going to cry.

Okay, that was a problem. "Look, I can set up electronic payments for you." Then I remembered they had no computer. "Or I can write the checks and you can sign them. I take care of the bills at home. We'd never have power if it were up to Dad. He always forgets."

"I didn't forget," she said quietly. "Mike, would you check the mailbox?"

"Okay." Sure, whatever it took to get this show on the road. I walked the obstacle course of water buckets in the front yard to the Harley-Davidson mailbox.

There was a Love Connection dating survey, a flyer from a local shoe store, and two envelopes stamped Past Due from Penn Telecom and Allegheny Power.

I walked slowly up the steps to Moo, who was standing at the front door, tugging her HOLY COMFORTER hoodie around her. "Are the Social Security checks there? They both should've come yesterday."

I shook my head and handed her the pile. I knew what *Past Due* meant. We'd gotten enough of those before I set up electronic payments for Dad.

She took the mail and walked into the kitchen.

I was slowly starting to figure it out. Collecting water in buckets in the front yard? Running out of gas? Watching imaginary movies in Tyrone? Why hadn't Dad told me they were poor? Probably because he was clueless. Then I realized something else. Dad had forgotten to give me the emergency money he'd promised. Now I couldn't even help! I pulled my wallet out of my back pocket and checked inside. Only twenty-seven dollars. I looked at Moo, helpless.

She held the opened electric bill in one hand and patted my back with the other. "It's all right, Mike. We have flashlights and a camp stove. We can go for quite a long time without power. We've done it before."

"How long?"

"Oh, weeks at a time."

"Weeks? We don't have weeks! We've got to get this artesian screw off the ground—or into the ground—or wherever it goes."

She stared up at me through her big owl glasses, her eyes cloudy.

"We need power! Power tools don't work without electricity!"

"True." She looked through the pass-through at Poppy. "But he's not working so well, either."

She was right. We had two problems: powerless tools and powerless Poppy. I could handle getting electricity for the workshop, but I wasn't sure how to get Poppy plugged in.

I took the electric bill out of her hand and looked for a phone number. There it was, next to their slogan, You Have the Power! "I'm calling the electric company and seeing if I can negotiate a deal to get them to turn on the power."

"That won't work, dear."

"Sure it will." I picked up the phone. "Every power company has an assistance program to help people who can't pay their bills." I shook the handset. "What's wrong with this phone?"

"That's what I mean, dear. It doesn't work."

I stared at her.

"The phone always gets cut before the electricity."

I slowly hung up the receiver. How long had they lived this way? I thought about what to try next. I really wished Dad had let me bring my phone. "Okay. Here's what we'll do. We'll drive over to the electric company—"

"But Tyrone's out of gas, remember?"

I groaned. "What about that Suburban in the driveway?"

She shook her head. "That's Poppy's. It doesn't work."

Like Poppy. "Look. I'll make you a deal. I'll go take care of the electric bill if you'll work on . . . giving Poppy a little charge."

5

COMPATIBLE NUMBERS

—numbers that group together easily and are easy to work with

It was a great plan, except I forgot one thing. I'm lousy at remembering directions, even in a small town like this. That's part of my dyscalculia. I couldn't find Allegheny Power. I did find a Shop 'n Save, though, and remembered what Moo said about scrapple being the only thing that kept Poppy alive, so I bought some. I had to. It was my only hope.

It took a while to find the scrapple, though, because I combed the cereal aisle before the manager asked if she could help me, and then busted out laughing when I told her. How was I supposed to know that scrapple is meat? I bought five pounds of the stuff. That was another bad plan, because whoever said rural Pennsylvania is cooler than D.C. must not have been here during a June heat wave. Sweat was running down my arms and legs like I'd been in PE for the last hour. I could only imagine what was happening to the scrapple.

Finally, I saw a sign of hope at the next corner. You Have the Power! Yes! It was the power company's slogan. I ran down the block, the bag of scrapple banging against my leg. I wheeled around the corner and saw the rest of the sign. You Have the Power! Build a Family, Adopt a Child!

What? I looked closer at the building. It was a warehouse or something. I looked down the street. No sign of anything like an electric company. Across the street was a park.

I put my bag down and groaned. The only other person on the street was a homeless guy, digging around in his shopping cart. I wondered if he knew where Allegheny Power was. Why would he? It wasn't like he had electric bills to pay.

I couldn't help staring at him, though, because I've always kind of identified with homeless people. I know that sounds weird. I have a home. I even have a family. Although Dad's more like a widower who happens to have a son. A son whose face he can't picture and whose name he can't remember.

Maybe I think about homeless people a lot because of what Dad always says. *If you can't solve the simplest problems, you'll end up on the street.* I often wonder if that's where I'll end up. What's it like to have no home? And no family?

The man looked up. He had dark bushy eyebrows and his face was bony and had stubby hairs on it like he hadn't shaved. But he had kind of a rock-star face, the type girls would chase after. Except that he was a homeless dude. And old. Probably forty.

He eyed my Shop 'n Save bag. "Is that food for the soup kitchen?" He pointed to the building I'd thought was the electric company and I saw another sign: Soup Kitchen 12:00–2:00 P.M. "Because it's after hours."

I shook my head. "I'm trying to get to Allegheny Power."

"Corner of Bartlett and Main."

"Right, but how do I get there?"

He gave me a whole list of directions, and as usual, they all left my brain as fast as he said them. I wished I'd brought a pencil and paper.

"Thanks." I picked up my bag and walked off like I knew where I was going. All the lefts and rights were jumbled in my head and I had no idea how I was going to get there. When I got to the corner, I started to turn left.

"Hey, kid!" he shouted. "I said right turn, then two blocks and turn left! Got it?"

"Yup. Thanks. Uh . . . how many blocks again before I turn right?"

He shook his head and grabbed his shopping cart. "I'll show you—wait a minute." He called across the street to the park. "Hey, Tresa!"

One of the moms looked over and waved.

"What time does Allegheny Power close?"

The woman looked at her watch and called back, "About five minutes ago!"

I let out a groan. "Oh, great! Now I'll never get the electricity turned on."

"Turned on where?" he asked.

"At my great-aunt and -uncle's house."

He examined me for a moment. "Mike?"

I stared back. "How did you know?"

He rubbed his forehead, distracted. "It's a small town." He jerked his head in the direction of the park. "Come on over to my office. Let me see if I can help get their power back."

I didn't see how he could help me with anything, much less getting power. Still, there was nothing else to do and I figured it was safe, what with other people in the park. I followed him as he pushed his cart across the street. The contents jiggled and clanked like a muffled load of recycling. He headed toward a park bench with a newspaper on it.

"Is that your office?" I asked.

"That? Are you kidding? Of course not."

He walked his rattling cart behind a freshly painted green bench, took off his jacket, and draped it over the front end of the cart. "This is my office. Have a seat." He reached over to his cart and pulled out a cell phone. "Tresa! What's Allegheny's number?"

My mouth dropped open. I'd never seen a homeless guy with a cell phone.

He looked at me and shrugged. "What? Tresa's dad used to work there, so she knows the number by heart." He dialed and eventually got a human and, with some very choice words, demanded "crisis assistance" because of an emergency situation at 517 North Poplar with elderly people and a child they were having to care for—me,

I guess—and yes, he'd accept twenty-four hours if that was all they were willing to give. He closed his phone and put it back in the cart.

"You'll need to get payment to them by the end of the day tomorrow, but at least you've got power until then."

"Thanks. I'll take it from here." Not that I knew how, but at least I had a grace period.

"No sweat." He pulled at his shirt collar. "You thirsty?"

I nodded, looking around for a water fountain.

He reached behind him and pulled a bottled water out of a cooler in his cart and handed it to me.

"Wow! It's even cold!"

"Yes," he said. "Ice has a way of doing that." He looked at my bag. "Do you have anything perishable in there? If so, you can put it in the cooler."

"That'd be great." At least until I figured out what I was going to do next.

He took the bag from me and put it in his cooler. "You hungry?"

"Starving," I said, wondering what else he had in that cooler.

Reaching into his cart, he pulled out a brown paper bag. "Take one."

I wasn't sure I even wanted to look in the bag, never mind eat anything that was in there. "I—I don't want to take your food. I mean, what if you want it later?"

But he practically shoved the bag into my hands. "People give me more than I can eat. You're welcome to whatever you want."

My stomach was growling at the mention of food, so I opened the bag, relieved to see prepackaged bars inside, all pretty boring looking except for a bright Twinkie package that stood out from the rest. I hadn't had one of those since . . . probably preschool or kindergarten. I remember my mom packing me a special snack and it had a Twinkie in it. I took it, almost reverently, and handed him back the bag.

"What!" He grabbed the Twinkie from me, his eyes wide, fixed first on the Twinkie, then on me.

"Okay, okay! I'll pick something else."

He didn't answer but ran with the Twinkie like it was on fire, reaching an overflowing trash can on the corner and stuffing it far inside, as if smothering it. His eyes blinked rapidly as he walked back.

"I thought you said I could have anything."

He shook his head. "I don't know how that piece of trash got in there."

"I would've eaten it!" My mouth was still watering for it.

"I know. That's why I tossed it. I'm saving your life."

"What, it's a killer Twinkie?"

His piercing eyes narrowed. "Partially hydrogenated fats. You eat them, you'll die an early death. I never let them pass my lips."

How could a homeless guy be so picky? "So what do you eat?"

"I like a nice piece of fresh trout with just a touch of lemon butter, some organic broccoli, and maybe a little brown rice, but I could probably make do without the rice."

I stared at him. He was as crazy as Poppy and Moo. Now he was grimacing at his hands.

"Can you get me my hand sanitizer?" he asked.

"Uh . . . sure. Where is it?"

"In my cart. Where else would it be?"

I saw a large bottle of hand sanitizer, but I didn't grab it right away because I was curious about what else was in his cart. Mostly it was boxes and coolers, but there were also stacks of brochures covered with plastic bags so I couldn't read what any of them said. I didn't see any clothes or a sleeping bag or stuff that you'd think a home-less person would need to live on. Where did he sleep? Or take a shower? Or go to the bathroom? I always wondered that about homeless people.

"Any time you're ready," he said, holding his palms out flat in front of me.

I was still holding the brown paper bag that used to have the Twinkie, but with my other hand I squirted some goop into his palms, which he proceeded to rub to-gether furiously.

"Okay," he said, taking the ex-Twinkie bag from me and rummaging in it for a moment. "Here." He handed me some sort of dark brown bar. "It's low glycemic, high protein, nice amount of fiber."

He was staring at me, so I had to open it and take a bite.

"How is it?"

"Kind of . . . cement-ish," I answered, my mouth working hard on chewing.

His mouth twitched almost into a smile. "Keep it moving, then, so it doesn't harden."

"Thanks . . . what's your name?"

"Just call me Past." He put the bag back in his cart.

"Past?"

"It's a nickname. So why are you here, Mike?"

"I told you. I was looking for the power company."

He tilted his head and stared at me. He had big brown eyes that looked kind, knowing, even sympathetic. His voice was soft. "No, I mean, what's your story?"

"My story?"

"Everybody's got one." He gave a little smile, not to me in particular, more like he was remembering something that was kind of happy but kind of sad, too. That rock-star image of him came to mind again, but it was of a serious rock star like Bono, who went around saving starving children and doing good stuff like that. "So, Mike, what's your story?"

I don't know why—maybe I was tired, maybe the heat was making me delirious, maybe it felt good to have someone to talk to—but I spilled my guts. About crazy Moo. Poppy, the wax figure. Felix, the dead cat clock. Tyrone, the dead car. Trying to get the electricity turned back on so we could get working on a special project, but the garage, excuse me, *workshop* was dead. And about how critical this project was but how I wasn't even sure it was going to happen. Which really sucked because that pretty much ruined my high school career and maybe the rest of my life. It was the kind of story that would've been embarrassing to tell anyone except a homeless person.

Past nodded and was quiet for a while. "You know why Poppy's like that, right?" Past started blinking fast. "Doug—his son—died."

"I know, and no offense, but it's not like Doug was a kid. He was already an old man."

"True, but I suspect Poppy is remembering Doug as a boy and feeling guilty about a lot of things. Poppy was one of those old-fashioned dads who didn't interact much with his son. Do you know the type?"

"Yeah," I said. I knew the type, all right. "Still, Poppy needs to snap out of it."

Past stared at me, still blinking, his voice grim. "It's not that easy."

"I'm not saying it's easy, but look at Moo. She's not sitting around like a vegetable while someone else does everything for her." The more I thought about Poppy, the more he reminded me of Dad. I wished there were some way to contact him. I had to get some money for Moo. Wait! "Past! Can I borrow your cell phone? I need to get in touch with my dad."

"Sure." He reached into his cart and pulled it out.

I tried calling Dad's cell, unsure if it worked over in Romania, but I got his voice mail and left a message to send money fast. In case he didn't check messages, which he often didn't—I usually had to leave several before he answered—I also sent a text. There was so much to say, I didn't know where to begin, so I just went with the bare essentials.

Dad—Poppy and Moo r POOR! Pls send money
fast—Mike

I handed the phone back to Past. "Thanks."

"No problem. I'll call Moo when I hear from your dad."

"Moo's phone isn't working."

"What about her cell?"

I gave him a give-me-a-break look.

"Not working, either? Well, check back with me here, then. I'm usually in my office. I spend the nights here, too." He said it so matter-of-factly, like he was one of those big law firm attorneys who work around the clock. Except his office was a park bench.

He stood up. "We should get you back to Moo. She may be starting to worry."

I got up, too, and watched as he picked his jacket up off the cart and put it on. I was stunned that he would want to wear a jacket when it was still so hot. But I was even more stunned to see what was now visible on the front of the cart where his jacket had been draped. It was a photo. Of a boy. Who looked just like me.

6

COMMON FACTOR

—a factor that two or more numbers share

Cute kid, huh?" Past said as I continued to stare at the photo.

I nodded. Piercing eyes. Like mine. Pale brown hair, what there was of it that you could see, because he had an almost-buzz cut. His mouth was open just a little, like he was trying to smile, enough to show a missing front tooth. And he was wearing my shirt.

"That's my T-shirt," I finally managed to say.

"I sincerely doubt that," Past said.

"It is! It's my Buzz Lightyear shirt!"

"Uh-huh," Past said, not sounding convinced.

I couldn't take my eyes off the photo. "And he looks just like me."

"He looks nothing like you."

"He's wearing my shirt! And—and he's got a tooth missing in front! Just like I had!"

"He's six, Mike. Every six-year-old has front teeth missing."

"True. But still, that's my shirt! Or it used to be. I had one just like that."

"Given that Buzz Lightyear is a Disney character, I would wager that there was more than one made in the world."

"Yeah, but—"

"And this boy lives in Romania, so—"

"Romania? That's where my dad is! And that's where my shirt went! I think."

"Excuse me?"

"Yeah, Sasha's—my friend's—church collects old clothes and sends them to eastern Europe. The kids' clothes go to orphanages. That's my shirt! I mean, think about it, how many Buzz Lightyear T-shirts could there be in eastern Europe?"

"Oh, I don't know . . . hundreds?"

"No! That one's probably mine."

I heard a gasp from Past. I looked at him. His eyes were wide. Finally, he was seeing the significance. Then he let out a yell. "Look out!"

He grabbed me and pulled me behind the cart.

Tyrone came barreling up on the sidewalk near the bench and jerked to a halt.

I felt Past release his grip. "It's okay." He exhaled. "She stopped."

"There you are, Mike!" Moo called, getting out of Tyrone. "I've been looking all over for you."

"Moo! How did you get gas?"

Moo clutched Junior and grinned. "I siphoned some out of Poppy's car. Don't tell him! But I had good news, so I just had to come find you." She pulled two envelopes out of Junior's outside pocket. "Look! My next-door neighbor admitted that she was—uh—*borrowing* my Oprah magazine that was put in her mailbox by mistake. I can't blame her. Who doesn't want to read *O*? But then she found our Social Security checks inside the magazine and came running over. So now we can pay the bills! The bank and the electric company are closed, but if we hurry, we might get to the phone company in time and we can talk to them about getting service back." She turned to Past, who was handing me my Shop 'n Save bag from his cooler. "Would you like to come with us, dear?"

Past took a step backward. "No. Thanks. Listen, are you sure you should be driving? You look a little . . . tired."

Moo glared at him. "Of course I look tired. That's perfectly normal when you're old as the hills. Goodness, most people my age are dead!" She grabbed my arm. "Come on, now, Mike, hop in!"

Tyrone lurched and I waved out the window to Past and took a last look at the little kid on his cart who looked like me. And I realized I had never asked him who the kid was or what he was doing on his shopping cart like a poster for a missing child.

"Hey, Moo, have you seen the picture of that kid on Past's cart?"

"Oh, yes. Isn't he sweet? He's coming here."

"From Romania?"

She nodded, smiling. "We're adopting him."

I stared at her. "You and Poppy?"

"Oh, no, it's a team effort."

"Who's on the team?"

"The whole town!"

"The whole town is adopting a kid?"

"You've heard that it takes a village to raise a child, haven't you?" She looked over at me and grinned. "Well, not really, but it feels like that. We're all trying to raise money."

"Cool. My best friend, Sasha, was adopted from Russia."

"Then you know all about adoption!"

"Well, not *all* about—"

Tyrone lurched to a stop in front of a strip of stores with glass fronts, mostly abandoned except for the phone company.

Moo peered at the door. "Oh, dear. They're closed, aren't they?"

My head flopped back onto the headrest. "Great. Now we have no phone service, either." And I'd need to make several more calls before I could be sure that Dad would actually check his phone.

Moo patted my arm. "I'm so sorry, dear. I'm sure you want to talk to your dad. I wish my cell phone worked."

I jerked upright. "You have a cell phone?" Maybe Past knew more than I thought.

"Yes, Doug gave it to me for Valentine's Day, right before he—" She bit her lip and pulled her hoodie strings. She took a deep breath, blinked a few times, and added, "He even prepaid the bill for six months."

I counted the months on my fingers. "It's still under contract! Where is it?"

She pulled Junior onto her lap and dug around. "Here."

"Moo! This is a smartphone!"

"It is very stylish, isn't it?"

"No, I mean, this gets Internet and everything!"

She shook her head, started Tyrone, and pulled back on the road. "Doug didn't pay for that part because he didn't think we'd use it."

"Oh." I tried turning it on. "And it's dead. Do you have a charger?"

She looked doubtful. "If I do, it'd be in Junior. Why don't you take a look-see?"

I rummaged through O magazines, receipts, a thermos—"Coffee," Moo explained—granola bars—"I need to have my snacks, Mike"—Dentu-Creme, pens, tissues, even a trial-size bag of dog food—I didn't ask—before, amazingly, finding a car charger, which I immediately plugged in. Yes! A signal! I called Dad. No answer again. I left a message and texted but wondered if that would be enough. "I need to e-mail him."

"Okay, dear, you go right ahead."

"Uh, except I need to find Wi-Fi."

"Who?"

"Where's the library?"

"In Hedgesville, but it's not open now."

Of course. "What time does it open?"

"September."

"September?"

"It can't afford to operate during the summer and can barely stay open three days a week during the school year."

"That's crazy!" I guess my teachers were right. We *were* privileged. "Do you guys have a coffee shop or restaurant with Internet connection?"

She smiled. "Mike, the correct term is Internet buffet."

I stared at her. She was serious. "Actually, it's Internet *ca*fé."

She waved her hand. "*Buffet, café,* either way, it's food *and* the computer. No wonder you young people love it so much."

"Let's just drive around some neighborhoods." Someone had to have Wi-Fi.

Tyrone headed up and down streets, but no luck. It wasn't exactly a Wi-Fi kind of town. The few I did find were locked. I held the phone out of the window, trying to get closer to the houses we passed.

Finally, I looked down at the phone and saw an unsecured network: *AdamsFamily*. "Stop! I think I've got something!"

Not only did Moo stop, she ran around Tyrone to my door, putting one hand on it and raising the other high in the air. "Is that better?"

"What are you doing?"

"I'm being your antenna."

"But I don't need an an—"

"Hurry up, before my arm gets too tired."

"But—okay, fine."

I quickly started an e-mail, putting "FROM YOUR

SON" in the subject line so Dad would notice. Between the sender name "Mike Frost" and "FROM YOUR SON," he might actually realize it was me.

> **Dad! Dude! TURN YOUR PHONE ON! Check your messages! Send money fast! Your son, Mike**

"Okay, done."

Moo ran around and hopped back in the driver's seat. "What did your dad say?"

"Nothing yet."

She shook her head. "Well, I don't think it's such a smart phone then if you can't even get an answer."

We passed the Kmart, so I knew we were getting close to home, when Tyrone slowed down. "Oh, dear," Moo sighed. "GAS!"

"What, again?"

"Tyrone's not out of gas. It's me."

"You're out of gas? Or . . ." I moved closer to the door. "You have gas?"

"*GAS* is an acumen, Mike. The first letters stand for items on my to-do list."

"You mean *acronym*."

"That's it! *G* stands for Gladys, *A* stands for Allegheny Power—because I have to do both those errands tomorrow morning—and *S* stands for Shop 'n Save. I should've found a way to buy scrapple, at least, because we're all out and now I have none for Poppy's dinner."

I grinned and held up my five pounds of scrapple. "Don't worry, Moo, it's in the bag!"

"Mike, you are such a savior. Where would we be without you?"

Moments later, she sang, "Home again, home again, jiggity jog!" Yanking Tyrone's wheel, she careened into the driveway, spraying gravel everywhere. We were headed straight for the parked Suburban and we weren't slowing down.

"Whoa! We're going to hit the"—*Crunch!*—"Suburban!"

"Of course, dear. That's what bumpers are for. Besides, it's only Poppy's."

No wonder Poppy didn't like Tyrone. I got out of the car shakily and watched Moo navigating the buckets in the front yard. She stopped and said, "Karen's here! That's her scooter!"

"Who's Karen?"

"She's a teacher—"

"A teacher?" Oh, jeez, had Dad found a teacher in Do Over to tutor me all summer? It wouldn't be the first time. "What's a teacher doing here?"

"She's also our temporary minister. She's a teacher during the school year. I bet she's here to talk to Poppy about the artis—artees—arteedge—"

"Artesian screw?"

"That's it!"

I hoped Karen was as persuasive as one of those televangelists who got people to send them all their money and everything they owned. She'd need to be strong to deal with Poppy.

Moo must've been thinking the same thing. "If anyone can get through to Poppy, Karen can. And Oprah, of course, but I don't think she's coming." Moo ran up the front steps. Pushing the front door open, she turned to me. "Mike, Karen will need to rely on you for the artesian screw."

"Me? Why me? And what's Karen got to do with—"

But her little yellow sneakers had already disappeared inside.

7

FORMULAS

—equations describing certain relationships

Before I reached the front door, I heard a loud "Moooo!" When I walked inside, I found Moo hugging a large woman with even larger hair. Her dress was only a few shades redder than her hair.

"Mike," said Moo, "this is Reverend Valentine."

Valentine? I guess that would explain the red color.

"Oh, you can call me Karen! I'm so glad you're here to help Poppy, Mike."

I heard a grunt from Poppy's chair. He had a frown, or maybe I should say his usual expression, on his face and the stupid yardstick clutched in his fist.

Moo shook her head. "I'm afraid Poppy's still thinking about Doug." She sucked in her lips and pulled on her hoodie strings.

Karen heaved a big sigh and gave Moo a hug. "And the other guys are lost without Poppy. Looks like we're going to need a miracle to get Poppy moving."

Moo brightened instantly. "We *have* a miracle!"

Karen and I both stared at Moo. I wasn't ready for the word that came out of her mouth. "Mike!"

I stood there looking as petrified as Poppy, only my mouth was hanging open, as Moo told Karen about all my "miracles" to date: getting us out of the airport, making her cell phone work, and buying five pounds of scrapple.

"Uh, Moo, we have to talk."

"Yes, dear?"

"I can't run this project. I don't have a clue what to do. I'm just a kid."

She looked at me hard through her thick glasses. "And Poppy is an eighty-three-year-old geezer who's away with the fairies."

Okay, she had a point. But still. An engineering project? I shook my head. "I'm sorry, but that's . . ." I wanted to say *the craziest wacko idea of this century.*

Moo's face fell and Karen's hair drooped.

Karen turned around to face Poppy. "Come on, big guy! We have orders from all over the country!"

How many artesian screws was he making? I hadn't even seen one yet, let alone lots.

"You've got to get this artisan's crew together," Karen ordered.

"Artesian screw," I corrected her.

Karen laughed and slapped my back so hard, I almost fell into the coffee table. "He's a funny one, isn't he? Now, Poppy," Karen continued, "you've got to get started. You're in charge here! We're counting on you! Let's get to the workshop! How about it, big guy?"

An unearthly grunt came out of Poppy's chair. Karen took a step back. I looked over at Poppy. His eyes had changed. They were slits, accentuating his devil hair horns. And his hands were in tight fists, one of them clutching the yellow yardstick.

"I take it that's a *no*," said Karen.

There was a squeaky cry out of Moo. "I need to vacuum now."

Karen cringed. "Oh, dear, I'm so sorry!"

Moo ran past me to the front hall closet and pulled out a vacuum cleaner and started sobbing. Karen plugged the cord into the wall and Moo fumbled with the switch until it turned on with a roar and the stench of old dust.

As Moo vacuumed her way into the kitchen, Karen patted my shoulder. "It's okay," she shouted over the vacuum. "This is what she does because she doesn't like to hear anyone cry, even herself. She vacuumed for three days straight after Doug died. When I came to pick them up for the funeral, she was still vacuuming."

I looked over at Poppy. "What about him?" I shouted in Karen's ear.

She motioned for me to follow her out onto the front porch, where we could talk a little easier, as long as you didn't look down at the red and orange swirly carpet. "Poppy didn't even pick up his feet when she vacuumed around his chair."

"So he hasn't done anything since Doug died?" I asked.

"Not a thing. Not even a word."

"That's just weird."

"It's very upsetting to lose a child, no matter how old."

"Yeah, but what about Moo? She does everything around here and he just sits there!" I thought about Dad. And me. "It's not fair for one person to handle everything."

"I agree with you. But he'll come around. Soon, I hope."

I thought about Poppy the Giant Turnip. And Dad. And I wasn't so sure.

"Maybe you can help," Karen said.

"I wouldn't even know how to start this project."

"I meant maybe you could help bring Poppy around. But as for the project—"

"Forget that," I said, shaking my head. "I can't—"

"But I need your help!"

Why was an artesian screw so important to her? "I'm just a kid!" And not a very smart one, either.

Karen took my hand in hers and looked at me intently. "I want a child, Mike. You have to help me."

My eyes popped wide open when I realized the implications of her statement. For the third time in ten minutes, I squeaked, "I'm just a kid."

"I know! And I want to adopt one just like you. Is that too much to ask?"

"Adopt? Oh. No, that's not too much to ask at all. That's, like, totally reasonable."

"All I'm asking is for you to help out with our project."

"Okay, but what does building an artesian screw have to do with adoption, anyway?"

Karen's brow wrinkled. "Artesian screw?" She pronounced the words slowly. "What is that?"

"That's the big project Poppy's supposed to be working on!"

She tilted her head.

"Moo told me about it."

Karen was still staring at me like I was making no sense.

"You know"—I gestured toward the garage—"out in his workshop?"

"Oh! *Artisan's crew! That's* what Moo was saying." She laughed. "Sometimes she gets her words mixed up. Have you noticed that?"

"Yeah, I have. But . . . what's the artisan's crew?"

She patted my shoulder. "You know what an artisan is, right? It's someone who makes beautiful things with their hands." She looked at me expectantly.

I nodded slowly.

"Well, Poppy does fine woodworking and is supposed to be leading a whole crew of people in making wooden boxes for—"

"Wait. What? Boxes?" I said. "Boxes?"

She nodded.

Dad's artesian screw plan was rapidly unscrewing. "You mean it's not some kind of engineering project?"

Karen laughed. "Not even close!"

"But—I thought Poppy was an engineer. Like my dad."

She laughed again. "He drove a dairy delivery truck for sixty years."

I let out a long, slow breath. I couldn't believe it. That was it, then. There was no artesian screw. No engineering project. No escape from Newton High. I looked at the orange and red swirls, felt queasy, and slumped against the door until the vacuum banged into it.

I moved away and Moo pushed the vacuum onto the porch. She was still sniffling. Karen pulled me inside and shut the storm door as far as it could go with the vacuum cord underneath it. The noise muted slightly.

"Let me explain," Karen said. "The whole town is helping me in my adoption effort. Have you seen the signs, 'Build a Family, Adopt a Child'?"

I tried to nod but I was still too stunned.

"We have to work fast because the adoption laws in Romania are changing and—"

"Romania? Is this the kid on Past's cart?"

Her smile drew up her cheeks and accentuated her heart-shaped face. "Isn't he adorable? His eyes are so piercing." She clenched her hands together under her chin, almost like she was praying. "We need everyone's help. Whatever you can do to get Poppy moving would be wonderful. He was going to get two hundred dollars for each box, but now I don't know how we'll make up that money."

I wondered how good I could get at making boxes. "How many boxes do you need?"

"Well, Poppy and his crew were going to make dozens."

Dozens times two hundred dollars would be . . . "How much money?"

"For the whole adoption? Well, if you include airline tickets, staying in the country during the adoption process—about forty thousand."

I nearly choked. "Forty thousand dollars?"

"By July fifteenth."

"What! It's June twenty-second! That's only . . ."

"Three weeks and two days."

"Why so fast?"

"Romania is about to close down international adoptions."

"What do you mean, 'close down'?"

"They're changing the regulations, so they're putting all international adoptions on hold for—well, we don't know how long."

"So someone else could adopt him?"

"Possibly, but adoption isn't very popular in Romania. It's more likely that he'll just sit there for months—or years—until they open up to international adoptions again."

Karen went on to talk about her "baby," and the toys she'd sent him, and the room she'd gotten ready for him, while I stood there trying to get my brain to work. The kid could be stuck in an orphanage for . . . forever. With no family. Alone.

"Oh!" said Karen. "Here's the picture of him I got this morning." She reached into her pocket and pulled out a small photo.

"Look!" She put the photo in my hand.

I peered at it and gasped.

"I know," said Karen. "Isn't he sweet? He's playing with the LEGOs I sent him. See what he's making? It's a house, or maybe it's a garage? For his little cars there."

I shook my head slowly. It was like I was looking at myself. It wasn't a house. It wasn't a garage.

"What is it? What do you think he's building?"

"It's a bridge," I said quietly, not taking my eyes off the photo. A bridge. Like the bridge I'd made out of LEGOs for Dad. The one that made Mom call me a great engineer.

"Oh," she cooed, "he's building a bridge from there to here. He wants to come. Do you know"—her voice cracked and her eyes watered—"they showed him a picture of me and he said"—her voice cracked again—"he said . . . Mama!"

The vacuum buzzed in my ears while I stared at the kid and Karen broke down.

"I want him home," she cried. "I have to raise the money. We need to get Poppy moving. Somehow!"

I shoved my hand into the pocket with my LEGO brick and stared at the photo. "Don't worry," I said. "This kid is definitely coming home."

8

EVALUATE

—to determine the worth of; to appraise

IKE!" a voice screamed in my ear. "Are you feeling all right, dear?"

I opened my eyes to see Moo's huge glasses in my face. "I—I think so. Why?"

"It's so late. I thought you might be sick."

I sat up in bed. "What time is it?"

"It's after eight!"

"Eight? Eight in the morning?"

"Yes! Poppy and I have been up for hours."

"I usually sleep until eleven, at least."

She laughed. "Oh, Mike! You are so funny!"

I flopped back down in bed and closed my eyes. I'm a very slow riser.

"I'm making brunch for you," Moo said, her voice fading as she headed downstairs. "Then we'll go to the bank to deposit the checks so we can pay the electric bill . . ."

The electric bill! I opened my eyes and sat up again.

For the power tools for the artesian screw! Oh, wait. My head hit the pillow. The project that was—

I sat bolt upright. "Adoption!" I said out loud as I stumbled out of bed.

I tried to think of everything Moo had told me the night before, after Karen had to run to a meeting. How the whole town was involved in fund-raising for Karen's adoption because her husband died and she always did so much for everyone, anyway. How all the churches came together for this cause instead of having separate church bazaars, including the Baha'i and Hmong—or as Moo put it, "the Buy-high Temple and the Mung Dynasty"—oh, and also the Lutherans. How everyone was having bake sales and selling their wares at the Exxon flea market and donating the money to Karen. How after the adoption agency said it was okay to put up a picture of "that enchanting face," the excitement really started. Still, it was such a small town, and from what I'd seen, it wasn't a rich one. I tried to get contact information from Moo for the artisans, but she was reluctant to tell me because she didn't trust the guys—Jerry, Spud, and Guido—alone in Poppy's workshop. Guido? There was really a Guido? "Yes," she said. "He's a wonderful artist, but not the kind of artesian who can build things."

In spite of Poppy being deadwood, so to speak, I hadn't given up on lighting a fire under him. And if I couldn't get him moving, maybe I'd make the boxes myself. If I could get Guido to paint them, people might not notice how badly they were made.

And I had to reach Dad. I had to get money fast to pay

Poppy and Moo rent, or pay their bills, or buy the food, or something, because they could barely support themselves, let alone me. Plus, we should donate some money to the artisan's crew and to the adoption costs. Oh . . . that could mean Dad would find out there's no artesian screw. Okay, must choose my words carefully.

I ran to the bathroom and tried to take a shower, but the showerhead was missing. I wondered if that was something else they couldn't afford. I wet my head under the sink faucet, my only chance to keep my hair under some kind of control, and was vaguely aware of an odd smell. It wasn't a bad bathroom smell, just not the kind of odor you normally found in a bathroom. It smelled like . . . salad dressing.

I ran back to my room, Doug's room, and pulled on my usual uniform of band T-shirt—this time the Rolling Stones—and jeans, complete with LEGO in the pocket.

"I'M GOING OUT TO TALK TO MY TOMATOES, MIKE! BRUNCH IS READY WHENEVER YOU ARE."

I heard the kitchen door slam and sat down on the bed to put my shoes on. Most people shove their feet into their shoes without even untying the laces. Not me. Tying and untying shoes were my daily moments of Zen, the signal to wake up in the morning and wind down at night. Besides, it didn't take any longer than the foot-cramming method because I skipped the time it took to walk around awkwardly trying to shove my heel into the shoe.

It was while I was doing my shoe-Zen thing that it caught my eye. A photo of a kid a little younger than me and a guy who I figured was a thinner, younger, happier

Poppy, with no devil hair horns. I picked up the denim frame and peered closer. It was strange seeing someone who looked more alive in an old photo than in real life. What really hit me, though, was that Poppy and Doug were sitting high off the ground in a tree house. A really beautiful, awesome tree house. Given that Poppy was, supposedly, a woodworker, they must have built the tree house together. Sweet.

"I'M BACK, MIKE!"

I almost dropped the photo.

I ran downstairs to find Poppy still sitting in his chair with the yardstick across his lap, like he'd never left. "Good morning!" I said.

Nothing.

I decided I wasn't taking nothing for an answer. The man had to snap out of it. And fast. "GOOD MORNING, POPPY!"

At least I made him flinch, even though he only gave a mild grunt in response.

I grunted back and went into the kitchen.

Moo pointed to a plate on the table. "There's your scrapple, dear."

Beyond the greasy sausage smell was that salad-dressing smell, even stronger than in the bathroom. It made more sense in a kitchen, though. I lifted the lid off a boiling pot on the stove and found the showerhead. I stared at it for a moment, not sure what to think.

"I'm cleaning it. Vinegar works wonders on lime deposits."

"Vinegar? It smells like salad dressing."

"I put herbs from my garden in it. Marjoram for the bathroom and oregano for the kitchen. Felix doesn't like scented vinegar, so I just put a drop of the plain stuff in his water. Did you know it kills fleas?"

I turned to stare through the pass-through at the cat clock. "No, I didn't."

"Vinegar has so many uses. I use it in my laundry. Soon your clothes will smell of vinegar."

I looked down at my Rolling Stones "Start Me Up" T-shirt and tried not to grimace.

"In fact, I'm going out to clean Tyrone's dash while you eat." She gave me a knowing smile. "Vinegar keeps plastic from getting dusty. It's great for so many things."

"Gee, Moo, you sound like an infomercial."

She laughed and headed for the front door, stopping to turn to me. "Oh, and if you get stung by a bee, you know the solution for that, right?"

"Vinegar?"

"That's it!" She walked out the door.

"Hey, Moo! You could sell vinegar to make adoption money!"

She popped her head back in. "Do you really think so? Well . . . I sell my tomatoes at the Exxon flea market. I suppose I could sell my vinegars there, don't you think?"

"Absolutely!"

"You're brilliant, kiddo!" Moo winked before disappearing with her vinegar.

Brilliant? Moo didn't know me very well. I sighed and took a bite of scrapple. And discovered that it's not half bad. It's all bad. "Hey, Poppy," I yelled, "how can you stand this stuff?"

He ignored me, of course.

"Do you want mine?"

No answer.

"Okay, I'm going to dump it in the trash."

His grunt was clearly audible.

"Fine, do you want to come in here and get it?"

No movement.

"Okay, this time I'll bring it to you, but next time you can get it yourself." I marched into the living room, grabbed the yardstick out of his hand—making him flinch again—and deposited the plate of scrapple on his lap. "Enjoy!"

I scrounged in the kitchen and found some generic Cheerios, which were okay, even with powdered milk. I was putting my cereal bowl in the sink and staring out the kitchen window at Moo's tomatoes, trying to calculate how much you could charge for each one, when she came back in.

"Isn't the lake beautiful?" she asked.

"What lake?"

"Lake Revival! Oh, you can't see it through all the trees at this time of year. It's where early settlers did their baptisms." She scrunched her shoulders up to her ears and grinned. "And it's where Poppy and I used to go skinny-dipping."

That was more than I needed to know. I shook my head to get rid of the image.

"Have some iced coffee." She handed me a glass full of ice cubes and an opaque beige liquid. "Chug it, and we'll hit the road."

I don't even drink coffee, but it was like drinking java ice cream, and I downed it all without stopping. Then I shivered because of the taste or the iciness, I don't know which.

Moo grinned. "Double caffeine, extra sugar. How do you think I stay so young?"

She headed out the door before me, so I was able to say a special good-bye to Poppy. "If you don't do anything in your workshop"—I took the workshop key off the rack by the door and paused for dramatic effect—"*I* will."

The loudest grunt I'd heard so far.

9

MIXED NUMBERS

—numbers that have both a whole
number and a fractional part

yrone parked in front of the bank, a little brick
building that looked like a cottage. There were
even window boxes out front with plastic flowers
in them. And a sign on the door that said, Build a Family,
Adopt a Child. With a poster of the kid's face. And those
haunting eyes. It looked like he was trying to say something, but I didn't know what.

"Isn't he adorable?" Moo said. "Gladys is fully behind this adoption. It's almost like she's the one adopting
him." Moo paused, her hand on the bank door, and sighed.
"Family is just that important to her. Oh, and you should
see the bling she knits to make money for the adoption."

Excuse me? "Bling?"

"Yes, dear. That means shiny, fun stuff. She knits all
kinds of beads and sequins into her scarves, hats, and
sweaters. They're beautiful." Moo opened the bank door.

"Where does she sell them?"

"At the flea market. And Big Dawg's. Her stuff is hot with bikers and bands. She can hardly keep up with demand. Now, Mike," Moo said, leading me over to a couple of flowered chairs in front of a desk, "come meet Gladys."

Gladys had six earrings, a pierced cheek, a tongue stud, spiked hair, and a leather skirt so short, I couldn't take my eyes off of it and the parts of her it wasn't covering. She did not look like a Gladys.

Moo sat down next to her and patted her hand. "Hello, dear. I'd like you to meet my grandnephew, Mike."

I stared at Gladys. She was drop-dead gorgeous. "H-huh—hi," I stuttered. "I hear you make b-buh-bling." I sounded like an idiot!

But Gladys smiled, making her appear almost normal. Somehow it made her black makeup and spiked hair seem softer. She held her hand out and I saw it was covered with tattoos, including a really cool one of a guitar that I was eyeing until Moo's hand clamped down over it. "Goodness! You've added some, dear, haven't you?"

"Yeah, it was after the breakup and then . . . well, we're back together again."

Moo did not look happy. "Numnut?"

"It's Num*chuck*, remember? Because he likes martial arts."

Moo sat up straight and sniffed in hard. "Well, if he tries any of that stuff on you, remember what I told you about where to kick him."

She grinned and nodded. "Right in the crotch."

I slid down into the other chair and crossed my legs.

"Here are some checks, dear. Please put them in my account right away because I'm already late."

"You should use direct deposit," Gladys said. "Then there'd be no question about it getting into your account on time."

"I don't trust those little computer elves. They might run off with my money." Moo put the electric and phone bills down on Gladys's desk, then started bragging about me for joining the adoption effort.

I saw a photo of the Romanian orphan on Gladys's desk. Even the crystal-studded, totally blinged-out frame couldn't take away from his questioning eyes. What was he searching for?

"Mike is very clever." Moo nodded knowingly at Gladys. "Just like you. I really wish you'd take some classes at the community college."

"I've already made assistant manager and I just graduated from high school this month," Gladys said defensively.

"That's what I mean, dear—you're so smart." Moo squeezed her hand and leaned in toward her. "You know I'll always love you no matter what you choose to do. It's just that you're such a clever girl. Like Mike. I think you're both ET."

"You mean GT?" Gladys said. "Gifted and talented?"

"That's it!"

I groaned inside. I hated the GT kids. It felt like every one of them knew that Dad was always trying to get me into GT even though I didn't have the brains for it. With a last name like Frost, I guess it was easy for them to come up with "Brain Freeze" as my nickname. I wanted to yell at them, "Hey, *I'm* the reason you're 'above average.' You should be *thanking* me!"

I looked at the other sign on Gladys's desk: We Promise You Absolute Value! Absolute value? That was the only math term I understood. It's when you take something that's worth less than zero, a negative—kind of like me—and it becomes positive. I always liked that idea. It was as if there were hope, even for me.

Moo squinted at the tellers behind the counter, leaned toward Gladys, and whispered, "New Dum Dums?"

"Moo!" I said, avoiding the eyes of the tellers she'd just insulted.

"She means the bowl of lollipops," Gladys explained. "Moo, go on and take a few. I know there's at least one root beer pop in there."

Moo jumped up, scurrying over to the counter.

Gladys gave me a serious look. "Does Moo still have that cell phone from Doug?"

"Yes. Why?"

Gladys picked up one of the bills and rubbed her forehead. "She can't pay both of these bills, and I think it's more important for her to have power."

"What do you mean? It's only two bills. And she just got Social Security checks."

Gladys crossed her arms and started rocking. "I know, but most of it will go to what's past due, and the next electric bill hits on Tuesday. I wish I got paid sooner. Then I could help."

"It's okay," I said quickly. "I'm getting money from my dad. How much does Moo have?"

Gladys eyed me, then Moo, who was still rifling through the bowl on the counter. "It's confidential, but I suppose if your dad is sending money, anyway, and you're family . . ." She turned the screen toward me.

I examined it, just like I did with our bank back home, ever since I was nine years old. What a joke—the kid with dyscalculia taking care of a bank account! The manager at our bank thought it was so cute, but, hey, if your dad isn't checking to see if there's enough money in the account, somebody's got to. The only difference between Moo's account and ours was the number under *Total*. Hers didn't have enough to buy a used iPod.

Moo appeared at Gladys's desk. "Oh, good! I see you met Mac. Gladys, can Mike send a message to his dad all the way in Romania on Mac?"

Gladys typed rapidly, then handed me the keyboard. "Sure."

"Moo, what's your account number? Dad's going to put some money in it."

Gladys froze.

So did Moo. Her voice was cold, too. "I don't need charity, Mike. I'm just fine."

Oops. "Uh . . . it's for me," I said, looking at Gladys for help.

"For your allowance, right?" Gladys nodded.

"Right! And also my birthday." In November. "Plus, we can buy more vinegar."

Gladys gave me a funny look.

"It's for making different flavored vinegars for Moo to sell and make money for the kid Karen's adopting."

Gladys brightened. "Oh, excellent idea!"

Moo clutched Junior on her lap, absentmindedly opening and closing the buckle. "Well . . . all right, I suppose. It's for a good cause."

Gladys had opened a browser, so I accessed my e-mail account. As I was typing, I glanced at my inbox of unread messages. One of them was from Dad! I opened it quickly.

> While in Romania, Ferdi has advised me to use AIM, otherwise known as "instant messaging." It will facilitate more timely communication. You may contact me at TheFerdiProfessor.

That was it. No response to my text or voice messages. Had he even seen them yet?

I stared at the message. I'd tried to get Dad to IM for three years, but he'd refused. *Instant messaging? Uh . . . Mike . . . that sounds like instant coffee. No taste. No thought. If you have something worth saying, it should be well thought-out.* Of course, I hadn't put it in terms he could understand, like "It will facilitate more timely communication." I'd said, "It's faster." Stupid me. I guess now that he'd heard it from a reliable source, like a Romanian university department or something, he'd do it.

I got on AIM and saw that he was logged on, so I started typing immediately.

> **Hey, Dad, it's Mike. Yeah, I know all about "instant messaging." I've been IM'ing for years. Glad you've joined the club. What is Ferdi, anyway? The university?**

Ferdi, short for Ferdinand, is my grad student. He's finding some particularly challenging problems to send you.

Right away, I decided I didn't like Ferdi. His name,
his job, and his need to find me particularly challenging
problems.

My fingers jammed the keys so hard, I kept making
mistakes and it took me forever to spit out:

So what about the money?

Money?

Dad, didn't you get my voice mail and text?

Oh, was that you? I turned my phone off. What is the
problem? Plane delayed?

**No, Dad. I've been here since yesterday.
The problem is Poppy and Moo. They have no
money. You've got to send some fast!**

I suspect you are unused to the limited amenities.

**What amenities? Seriously, Dad, they have
no money. Moo had to siphon gas out of another car!**

Hyperbole has its use in literature but I'm very busy.
Briefly tell me what you need.

$$$$

No. I need an actual explanation.

**Actual explanation: They can't afford to buy
groceries. Their power keeps getting cut.
They have no phone service. Moo really did
siphon gas out of another car. They drink
powdered milk.
And you forgot to give me even the emergency money!**

I believe you may be right about the emergency money and I see there are financial difficulties. I can wire money directly to their account but it is ONLY for dire emergencies.

Aw, and we were planning to blow it all at Big Dawg's Tattoo and Bar, and then go skinny-dipping in Lake Revival.

There was no typing on the other end. I asked Gladys if I could call Dad for bank business—just long enough to leave Moo's account number. Of course, he didn't answer. His phone was still turned off, so I sent another IM.

I left a voice mail with her account number. Please listen!

Must teach class. Next message, report on artesian screw.

The artesian screw? Oh, crap.

"Are you finished, Mike?" Moo asked.

"Oh, yeah," I said, my head drooping almost to the keyboard. "I'm totally finished."

10

REFLECTION

—a mirror image of a figure

I asked Moo to drop me at the park while she went to pay the electric bill. I had to see Past. There was something about him that made him seem like a counselor, like you could tell him anything, even though that sounds weird to say about a homeless guy.

"Hey, dude," I said, approaching his "office," where he sat reading *The New York Times*. I slumped down on the bench next to him. "'Sup?"

He folded the paper. "The usual mayhem and carnage. What's new in your life?"

I looked at the kid on Past's cart and sighed. "The usual mayhem and carnage."

He chuckled. "What could you have going on that's so bad?"

"Oh, gee, let's see. There's Poppy. No engineering project. My dad. Newton High. And a kid in Romania who might never find a home."

Past frowned, looking serious. "We're working on the adoption."

"Who's supposed to be making the boxes in Poppy's workshop?"

"That would be Poppy."

"No, I mean, other than Poppy."

Past grimaced. "Poppy was supposed to train the others. No one's nearly as good as he is. Not good enough to sell them."

"Well, that's just great. Karen needs *forty thousand dollars*! In *three weeks*!"

"I know."

Then I realized something I hadn't asked. "How much has she raised so far?"

Past lowered his eyes and spoke softly. "About . . . well . . . fifteen—"

"That's it? Fifteen thousand?"

"No. Fifteen hundred."

"What!"

"At last count," Past said quickly. "It might be a little more now. Maybe a couple of thousand."

I stood up and started pacing. "I've got to get Poppy moving."

"Is he seeing anyone? Like a therapist?"

I shrugged. "Karen's a minister, right? She came by last night."

Past raised his eyebrows.

I shook my head. "Nothing. I'm trying to get a rise out of him. I'm talking at him, but I wouldn't exactly call it a conversation."

Past's brow furrowed and he stood up, walking behind the bench to his cart. "Let me give you something." After a few moments of jiggling and clanking in the blue and white cooler, he pulled out a small brown bottle. He cleared his throat and reached his arm over to me. "Here, try this."

I took the bottle and read the gold label. "Saint John's Wort?" I'd seen this before. On our kitchen counter. Dad took it every day along with his Centrum Silver. "Thanks, but I don't think a vitamin is going to help much." I handed it back to him.

Past leaned his forearms on the cart handle. "It's not a vitamin. It's for treating depression."

Depression? I looked at the bottle again. It was even the same brand Dad used. "Is that all it's used for?"

"Depression and anxiety. There are other uses people have come up with, but none of them have been scientifically proven."

Well, Dad wouldn't use it for anything that wasn't scientifically proven, that's for sure. So it had to be depression or anxiety. I had no idea.

"Just take it and try it. But tell Moo to check with his doctor first and make sure it's okay for him. We can't assume that. Assumptions like that can be dangerous."

"Yeah, like I *assumed* Poppy was an engineer." I told Past about the "artesian screw" disaster.

A voice came from the next bench. "Did you ever look closely at the word *ASS-ume*?"

I looked beyond Past and saw three old guys sitting on the bench and did a double take. They looked like the

Three Stooges I'd seen in Sasha's dad's DVD collection. The one nearest us had a bowl-type haircut like Moe, the one in the middle had curly hair like Larry, and the chubby guy on the far side was bald. He'd be the Stooge called Curly, which is what I always got a kick out of because he was practically bald.

"*Ass-ume*," said the Moe look-alike, "is made up of *ass* and *u* and *me*."

"When you ASS-ume," said the Larry stooge, "you make an ass of you and me."

All three of the stooges laughed.

"Next time, be more careful. . . . What's your name?" the Moe character asked.

"Me? Mike."

"That's a funny name. Me-Mike. I'm Guido, this is Jerry, and the quiet one is Spud."

"These guys," said Past, "were part of Poppy's"—he coughed—"artesian screw project."

"Yeah, it's screwed, all right," said Jerry.

Spud nodded. So far, he hadn't spoken.

"Hey, Poppy lost his son," Guido said. "We need to give the guy some time."

"Karen doesn't have much time," I pointed out, looking at the photo on Past's cart again. What was the kid saying with those eyes? It was like he needed me. Or something. Well, I could at least try to help him while I was here, since there was no hope for me.

"We've got other tricks up our sleeve, right, Past?" Guido said. "Porch pals. They could bring in a ton of money for Karen's adoption."

I pulled my eyes away from the kid's. "A ton of money? Really?"

"Definitely," said Past. He closed his eyes, smiled, and let his head drop back like he was basking in the sun. "I love porch pals."

"What are porch pals?" I asked.

Guido startled. "What are porch pals? You're not from around here, are you, Me-Mike?"

"He's from our nation's capital, remember?" Jerry said.

"Which just goes to show you how out of touch those people are. A porch pal is like a large stuffed buddy. The guys and I"—he pointed to Jerry and Spud—"we make them ourselves. You put him on your porch. You put him in your car. You put him wherever you want."

I felt my heart sinking. It didn't sound like a "ton of money" kind of product. "Why would people buy them?"

"Why? You got an instant pal!" Jerry said.

"And people pay good money for them," Guido added. "I heard of one person in your area with a porch pal." He chuckled. "The guy uses him so he can take the express lane during rush hour because you have to have at least two people in your car. Cuts his commute time in half. Now, that's worth a lot of dough."

"How much do you sell them for?" I asked.

"About thirty bucks."

I tried to do the math. Thirty . . . they'd have to sell . . . way over a thousand. Was there a market for that many porch pals? "Where do you sell them?"

The three stooges looked at each other.

"That's the problem," said Guido. "The local market

is flooded . . . so to speak. The guys and I loaded up my school bus and drove a bunch of porch pals over to the Johnstown Flood Museum gift shop. But one of the volunteers freaked, saying they looked like bloated flood victims, so that's a no-go."

Jerry and Spud shook their heads sadly in agreement.

"Why don't you advertise and sell them on the Internet?"

"Good idea," Guido said. "I have no idea how you plan to do that, but go for it. Glad you're in charge."

"Me?"

Past seemed to snap out of his porch pal stupor. "That's an excellent idea!"

"I don't even know what they look like!" I protested.

Guido and Jerry eyed each other and both pointed to Spud, who smiled broadly.

"And just look how fun they can be!" Jerry said, moving Spud's arms and legs in various poses, even manipulating his face while Spud obligingly changed his expression.

My toes tingled and my brain started to kick in. Porch pals might actually appeal to some people. The three stooges didn't know how to sell online, Moo would have no clue, and I couldn't ask a homeless guy to do it, so it really was up to me. I could build a website . . . except I didn't have access to a computer . . . I could get to Facebook and MySpace on Moo's cell phone if we drove around and found working Wi-Fi . . . but that wouldn't reach as wide an audience . . . eBay? Craigslist? I'd have to open a PayPal account—again, I'd need computer access . . . YouTube? That could work. Buyers could send a check to Moo's address and we could mail them porch pals . . . of course, I'd need a camera and a way to upload a video—

"Incoming!" Spud shouted, startling me all the more since I wasn't sure he knew how to talk.

Past stood up quickly, pulling me behind his cart. "Take cover!"

Moo pulled up in Tyrone, jumping the curb, but not close enough to be threatening.

"Yoo-hoo! Mike!" Her little yellow sneakers ran over to the bench.

As soon as they saw Moo, all three stooges started mooing like cows.

"Hello, boys," said Moo, waving at them. "They're always doing that," she whispered to me. "I don't know why."

"They're being cows!"

"Well, I know that, dear. I just don't know why they do it, that's all."

"Because your name is—"

"Name! That's what I wanted to tell you! You'd better sit down, Mike. In fact, I need to hold on to something."

Past guided Moo over to the bench and sat her in his spot. She looked at his cart behind her and pointed to the photo of the Romanian orphan. "Do you know his name?"

I suddenly realized I'd never heard his name.

"That boy's name," said Moo, "is Misha. Do you know what Karen just told me?"

I shook my head.

Her owl glasses stared at me and she took a deep breath. "*Misha* means 'Mikey.' His name is Mike. Just like yours!"

I knew it! I stared at the photo of the kid—of Misha. I knew there was something special about him. Beyond his eyes and his missing tooth and my Buzz Lightyear T-shirt and the LEGO bridge. There were just too many coincidences. This kid was . . . just like me!

"It's a sign," I said.

"A sign?" Past said. "You just happen to have the same name. Michael is a common name in many cultures."

"But it's more than just a coincidence," Moo said. "Don't you think it's a miracle?"

"Not really," said Past. "If the name were something unusual, like Igor, that would be a miracle."

Moo glared at him and looked at the three stooges. "And here's another sign. Do you know who else was adopted from Romania? Mike's best friend, Sha-sha."

"Russia," I corrected her, "and it's *SA*-sha."

"Whoa, Me-Mike. You are a stud," said Guido.

"*SA*-sha is a guy!" I said.

Guido stared at me. "Strange name for a guy."

I stared back. "He's from Russia! It's not a strange name over there."

"Exactly," said Past. "Just like Misha is not a strange name over there."

Guido didn't blink. "What's your point?"

Past exhaled loudly. "Mike . . . Misha. Just a coincidence. Not a sign."

"I still think it means something," Moo said.

Past rolled his eyes. "It means you're all getting carried away."

The others argued as I stared again at Misha's eyes. Burning into me. I stuck my hand in the pocket of my jeans and felt the LEGO brick. It was strangely warm. Maybe because it was a warm day. Maybe because it was against my leg, which was also warm. Or maybe it really was a sign.

11

DEPENDENT EVENT

—an event whose outcome is affected by the outcome of previous events

Guido told Moo how I was going to "Internet the porch pals," adding, "I tell you what, I was beginning to lose hope. I mean, forty thousand dollars in three weeks seemed like a hopeless cause, but now that Me-Mike is here, I think we might actually save this kid."

"Heaven knows Karen deserves a child. Anyone who's been through the horror of three miscarriages and a dead husband like she has . . ." Moo shook her head and sighed. "Karen is always there for us, and now it's our turn to be there for her." Moo's owl eyes fixed on me. "I know you can do it, Mike."

I stared at Moo and the three stooges, nodding in the background.

I heard a quiet whistle from Past. "No pressure, though."

"Oh, of course not," Moo said. "We're all helping. It's not completely up to you."

"Uh, thanks," I managed, my throat dry. I quickly told Past my YouTube idea. "I need some decent video equipment. Fast. Do you know how I could get that?"

Past thought for a moment. "Moo," he called, "is it okay if I take Mike over to Dr. P?"

Moo looked at us, fingering her glasses. "Are you having eye trouble, Mike?"

Past shook his head. "We need to borrow his camera equipment. Mike's going to make some videos and put them on the Internet to make money for Misha."

Moo's owl glasses looked at me. "You know how to do that?"

"Sure."

Her eyes moved to Past. "See? There's another sign for you."

Past sighed, muttering, "If they were both named Igor, that would be a sign."

"Would you boys like a ride?" Moo asked. "I could drop you off on the way to my other errands."

"No, no, that's okay," Past said quickly. "I—I need to bring my cart." He looked at me. "Come on, Igor, let's go."

I followed Past and his shopping cart over crumbling sidewalks in front of derelict buildings. He slowed down in front of one store, Natalie's Natural Products, where there was a picture of Misha. His eyes were burning into my brain. I heard Past take a ragged breath and I tore my eyes away from Misha.

Past was blinking at the window. It was just the kind of store he'd like, being a health nut, but it was closed. In fact, when I looked closer, I saw it was out of business. I was about to point that out to him when I noticed how pale his face was. When he saw me looking at him, he shook himself, cleared his throat, and walked on.

Except for the park, and the occasional poster of Misha staring at us, it was a depressing town. And poor. No wonder they'd only raised a couple of thousand dollars. We had to reach a wider audience.

I looked at my feet to avoid the urban blight, and that's when I noticed Past's shoes for the first time. Brown leather Clarks. Like mine. How could a homeless guy afford Clarks? Maybe he just lucked out. Somebody bought the wrong size? Or outgrew them fast?

The last time Sasha asked me why I kept buying Clarks, I almost told him. But just as I was about to spill my guts, Julia Albasio giggled up to him and he was in girl heaven. The truth probably would've sounded stupid, anyway.

I'd gotten dragged shoe shopping with Dad when I was nine, and old Mr. Friedman at the shoe store said he remembered that my mom used to bring me in there. Suddenly it didn't seem so bad to be in Friedman's Shoes with my dad wondering out loud why on earth Rockport would've changed the style of the perfectly good shoes he'd bought four years ago. I sat on every one of the yellow plastic chairs because I thought, just maybe, my mom might have sat in one. I asked Mr. Friedman what kind of shoes my mom bought me. "Clarks," he'd said. "She was a smart lady, your mother." I'd followed him to the register like a stray dog looking for scraps. I knew so little about my mom. Dad never talked about her, so I was desperate to learn anything I could. "She came in one day when you were maybe two years old," Mr. Friedman told me, "and she says, 'I've done the research, and from now on, I don't want my son wearing any shoe but Clarks.'" I asked what color Clarks she bought me. "Sable," he said. "It's just brown, but they say sable, so they charge twenty dollars more." I didn't leave the store that day until Dad bought me a pair of brown lace-up Clarks. I hadn't worn anything but Clarks brown lace-ups since. Except for sports and PE. I mean, I'm not a total geek.

Past pushed his cart into a crosswalk and pointed down the street. "That's where we're headed. Eye Associates of Pennsylvania."

As we got closer, I confirmed what my eyes had first read:

YE ASS
OF PENNSYLVANIA

"It doesn't say 'Eye Associates.' It says—"

"I know. Talk to ye doctor about it."

I looked at the poster of Misha in the window as we walked inside. A stout bald man in a white lab coat rushed toward us from the back of the store. His glasses were so shiny, they reflected the front windows and the fluorescent lights in the ceiling. "Hello, Past! What a pleasure! And who's your young friend?"

"This is Mike, otherwise known as Igor"—I glared at him—"Moo's grandnephew."

He extended a hand to me. "I'm Dr. Perrello, two *r*'s, two *l*'s."

I shook his hand. "Mike Frost. Hi."

He smiled and began polishing the lenses of the sample frames on the rack along the wall beside us, without taking his glasses off of me. "Mike. Maybe I can enlist your help in getting Moo to come for a visit. She hasn't set foot in here for three years." The polishing cloth stopped for a moment and he lost his smile. "I'm a little worried about her." The cloth started again. "How is your eyesight? No problems as you're growing? That can happen in adolescence."

"No, I can see perfectly fine. In fact, I was looking at your sign and it says—"

He chuckled. "I know. To tell you the truth, I get a lot more business now than I did when it was correct."

"Business? People just walk in and decide they need glasses?"

"Not my business. My wife's. She sells fruit spreads and cakes. After the sign got . . . rearranged, she changed her label to 'Ye Ass Homemade Goods,' and business really picked up.

He pointed to the counter beside the cash register with a huge basket full of plastic-wrapped packages next to a pyramid of jam jars.

Past was over at the counter faster than a speeding shopping cart. "Lydia's fruit spreads are great!"

"Yup," Dr. Perrello said proudly, "all fruit, no sugar."

Past whistled, staring at a label. "Blueberry, huh?" He whipped his head around to face the eye doctor. "Fresh or frozen?"

"Fresh, of course." The doctor glared at Past over his glasses.

"Lots of antioxidants in blueberries." Past rubbed his chin. I started tapping my foot impatiently. "How much are they?" he asked.

"Four dollars."

Past dropped his head like a brick had hit it.

"Aw, go ahead and take one," said Dr. P. "Lydia would want you to have it. And take a couple of her fruit squares while you're at it."

"Hey," I said, seeing an opportunity, "would your wife like to sell some of those for Misha, the kid Karen's adopting?"

His eyes brightened through his shiny glasses. "She already is! She's made a modest amount at the flea market. The thing is, lots of people around here make their own jam, so there's not a huge demand."

"No problem. We can put them on the Web—eBay and anywhere else I can think of, like YouTube." I asked if we could borrow his video equipment and explained it all to him. How I was going to record videos of porch pals, vinegar, whatever we could, and appeal for buyers or even donations. The videos would be short so people would actually watch them, sort of like public service announcements. Only more desperate.

"You know who should go on the Web?" said Dr. P. "Gladys."

"Gladys from the bank?"

"She used to do solos in church when she was a tiny little thing. What a beautiful voice. I was always sorry she didn't keep it up. But her mother—I guess it was really her father's fault—well, anyway . . . maybe you could ask her, since it's for a good cause." His eyes landed on Past's cart. "Let me go get the equipment and load up the cart."

I walked over to Past, who was scrutinizing the ingredients list on a fruit square. "What's the story with Gladys?"

He didn't take his eyes off of the label. "Sugar—but she doesn't say what kind. Well, at least it's not high fructose corn syrup. That stuff means instant diabetes."

"Past. What were her parents like?"

"Stay away from that high fructose corn—"

"Hello! Could you answer the question?"

He looked up from the fruit square. "I don't know Gladys's story because I've only lived here a couple of years. I know she plays guitar and sings, that she has poor taste in men, and that Moo has tried to take her under her wing because Moo is this town's savior of lost souls, but I don't know Gladys's past, okay, Igor?"

Past finished rearranging the pyramid of fruit jars, now that he'd removed one, as Dr. P came out with an armload—camera, tripod, mikes, cables. "Happy filming!"

Past opened the blueberry jar before we were even out of the store. I stared at him as he slurped the spread right out of the jar and purple juice dribbled down his chin.

"Jeez, you attack it like my dad attacks a Snickers— like it's going to run away if you don't grab it."

Past eyed me from around the jar and slowly took it away from his lips. "Snickers have hydrogenated fat. He shouldn't be eating those."

"There's a lot he shouldn't be eating."

"Is he overweight?"

"Big-time."

"You've got to get him to go on a diet!"

"Oh, right, like he'll listen to me."

"You're his son. You care about him. Of course he'll listen to you."

I shook my head and continued pushing his cart.

"You have to try. Promise me?"

"Okay, fine, I promise. So, now that we've got the camera equipment, we need to find a laptop and somewhere that has a high-speed connection to upload the files."

Past used his finger as a spatula to get the rest of the blueberry glop. "I have Wi-Fi."

I eyed him. "Seriously?"

Past gave an overexaggerated sigh. "Oh, ye of little faith." Then he gave me a smile. "It's from the lawyer's office right by the park. Often people can get a signal, sometimes not."

I knew how to handle that. "I need a can of Pringles."

Past frowned. "Fruit would be a better snack."

"No, it's for a Wi-Fi antenna to get better reception. Sasha and I built one out of a Pringles can so we could use his neighbor's Wi-Fi." I explained how, and Past assured me he'd get all the parts I needed for the antenna if I agreed not to eat the Pringles.

We shook on it. "You are nothing if not resourceful, Mike."

I shrugged. "I still need a laptop to upload the pictures and videos."

"I'll ask if I can use the soup kitchen's laptop for the uploads."

"They have a laptop?"

"It's almost brand-new, just given to them by"—he started blinking rapidly—"someone . . . who wasn't using it anymore."

"I can design a website to raise money for Misha by selling Moo's vinegars, Mrs. P's fruit spreads, porch pals—"

"Porch pals?" He got that goofy look on his face that porch pals seemed to inspire in him, and nodded.

"Good. Now, I just have to think of a video that'll get people to buy porch pals."

"I'm sure you'll find some sign, Igor."

"Would you stop calling me that?"

Past sighed. "I guess I'll have to go back to calling you by that culturally common name of *Mike*."

"Look. I know you don't think it's a sign that Misha and I have the same name. And you have a point. But it's not just the name. Or the T-shirt. Or even the LEGOs. It's the eyes."

Past stopped the cart and studied me. "Yours are brown. His are blue." He paused. "They both start with *b*. Is that the sign?"

I folded my arms. "No. His eyes are . . . I don't know . . . trying to say something."

Past raised his eyebrows.

I pushed the toe of my Clarks against a wheel of his cart. "It's like . . . okay, this is going to sound really weird . . . it's like he's trying to tell me something."

Past's eyes were wide and his face was frozen.

"Never mind! Forget I said anything!"

"No." He started blinking again and leaned his forearms on the cart, bending over like I'd knocked the wind out of him. "I believe you, Mike," Past said quietly. "If you're feeling something at a gut level, then you know what? You're right. That's a sixth sense. Or spirit. Or whatever you want to call it." He looked up and stared at me with his Bono eyes. "I want that kid adopted, too." For a long moment, he just kept staring at me. Then he scratched his stubbly chin and a smile started growing until it was a broad grin. I realized that I'd never seen him smile this much, because now that I saw it, I knew for sure that he was a guy the girls would drool over. Jeez, why didn't I get his face? I mean, if I wasn't going to get a brain, couldn't I at least look good? Past even looked great in a frayed green-striped button-down shirt and tweed jacket. Maybe I should wear—

"My shirt!"

"What?" It came out croaky because I couldn't believe he'd been inside my head.

"My shirt! I can sell my shirt on eBay!"

I felt better realizing that he hadn't known what I was thinking, but it took me a moment to catch on to what he said. "EBay? A shirt?"

"It's not just any shirt. It's a shirt worn by a real street person."

"Don't you . . . need it?"

He waved his hand. "Plenty more where this came from. In fact, I'll put one shirt a week on eBay."

"Do you have that many shirts?" I asked.

He gave me a funny look. "I believe I can part with that many shirts, yes." He put the blueberry jar in his cart, whipped off his jacket, and unbuttoned his shirt, taking it off quickly. He handed it to me as he started to put his jacket on over his gray T-shirt with his free arm.

I was doubtful, but I decided to humor him. "Okay," I said, slowly reaching out for it, trying not to act like I didn't want to touch it. "Uh . . . I'll take care of washing it."

He jerked it back. "What? Are you crazy? And devalue it? This is a shirt worn by a real live homeless guy. This shirt has lived against the man's skin! This shirt has lived on the street, night and day, for . . ." He froze, went pale, and then slowly a look of resignation came over his face, gentling out the lines in his forehead. His voice came out low and in a monotone. "I've been forgetting to count. Wow," he said quietly. "Anyway, it's been"—he looked at his watch—"two months, twenty-seven days, six and a half hours."

"Since what?"

He blinked rapidly, not looking at me and not answering. "I—I have to get to the soup kitchen. In the meantime, I'll head you in the right direction for home."

12

ORDER OF OPERATIONS

—the order in which a problem is solved

I was a little frustrated that we couldn't get started on videos or website design right away, but I figured I couldn't begrudge a homeless guy a free lunch. Past told me how to get back to Moo's and drew a map on the back of a flyer from Natalie's Natural Products health food store. Those were the flyers he had in his cart, and for some reason he had a ton of them. I guess they weren't any use to Natalie anymore, since her store was out of business.

Fortunately, there was only one turn to get to Moo's, so even I could follow a map like that. It was still a long walk, but I had a lot to think about, so I made a list in my head.

Website—call it Bring Misha Home!

- *upload pictures of Misha and tell about his life—what it is now, and what it could be*
- *show countdown on website of how many days before Romania closes*
- *show running tally of how much money we've made and how close we are to the goal*
- *get Moo on camera selling her vinegar*
- *get Past on camera eating Mrs. P's fruit spread*
- *get Gladys on camera playing guitar and singing!*

And the list went on and on.

I was thinking so hard, I almost missed my turn. When I got to Moo's, I maneuvered around the buckets in the front yard and walked up the carpeted steps. And stopped.

A life-size rag doll sat on a chair on the porch. Wearing shorts and a striped T-shirt, like an overgrown kid. And a pink Life Is Good baseball cap. Its face was a round pale blue pillow with brown yarn hair. He had buttons for eyes, a dangly red pom-pom for a nose, and a wide, grinning mouth drawn on with black marker. It was so hideous that, well, it was kind of cute. I stared at it for a moment before I noticed the note sticking out of the shorts pocket:

Hey, Me-Mike! This is a porch pal.
He'll bring you good luck.

—Guido, Jerry, and Spud

I couldn't help smiling at him until I noticed the

smell. Coming from the house. It was sickly sweet. And burning.

I yanked the door open. "Moo!" I shouted.

"In here, Mike!" Moo called from the smoky kitchen.

Poppy grunted as I ran through the living room.

"Moo, what's going on? What's that smell?" On the kitchen counter, I saw four cookie sheets completely covered with thick, black, smoking glop.

Moo sighed. "These cookies are for a bake sale for Misha. They didn't turn out very well, did they?" She looked down at her recipe card and read off the items as she put her hand on each of the ingredients on the counter. "One cup of sugar, three cups of flour—"

"Moo?"

"Yes, dear?"

"That's not flour. You've got two bags of sugar."

She peered at the bags. "I could've sworn one of them was flour."

"Moo, maybe you need new glasses. Your eyes might be getting—"

"My eyes are perfectly fine!" she said, whipping her head around to glare at me.

"I'm just saying . . ."

Moo turned to glare at the cookie sheets instead. "Well, that was a bust! Never mind, I'll clean this up and get our meal started. You go relax with Poppy for a few minutes."

I went into the living room and frowned at Poppy. For the first time, I noticed his feet. He wore huge duck slippers. They were realistic-looking ducks, the type with the dark green heads and necks. Other than the duck slippers, and the yellow yardstick now leaning against his recliner instead of across the arms of the wing chair, nothing had changed. Except the cat clock, which now said 5:15. Before, it had read around 8:00. Weird. I looked at Poppy. He had the same stubborn expression and devil-horn hair. His eyes were still fixed on the broken TV.

"So, Poppy, what up?"

No answer.

"How are those boxes coming?"

Mild grunt.

"Yeah, well, that's not helping make any money to bring Misha here. Guess you don't care about that. It's more fun to watch a dead TV, huh?" I looked at the blank screen. "Is this your favorite show?" I cupped my hand to my ear. "What's that? Oh, it's a movie. My mistake. James Bond?"

Moo appeared in front of me. "What are you doing, dear?"

"Watching TV."

She walked over to the set and pressed a button, and a truck ad shouted at us. "It works much better if you turn it on."

Poppy let out a snort.

"But I thought—"

"It's all right." Moo patted my hand. "Sometimes I forget to turn it on, too."

"I didn't forget! I thought since Poppy was watch-ing . . . never mind." Why would I think that Poppy would want to watch TV "live" when he could watch it dead?

Moo beckoned me into the kitchen and I followed. "I'm not sure Poppy is the best role model for you," she said softly.

Poppy made a low growling sound.

I sneered through the pass-through at him. No kidding. He was ruining my life, at least for the short term, but more importantly, he was risking Misha's entire life.

"Now, that Past," she said, drying her hands on a towel, "he's an excellent role model."

"A homeless guy?" I liked Past a lot, but it seemed weird to call him a role model.

"Oh, he's not homeless, dear."

"Uh, yeah, I think he is."

"Why do you say that?"

"For starters, his office is a park bench. And he sleeps there, too."

"Oh, that." She stirred a pot on the stove. "It's summer. He likes sleeping out in the open air. He used to go camping a lot, you know."

"He eats at the soup kitchen."

"No, he's just there a lot because he likes to volunteer his time."

"Moo. He pushes a grocery cart around town. Doesn't any of this sound strange to you?"

"We all need a place to put our things. I put everything in Junior. He has a lot of important things in that cart. Mike, could you hand me the parsley flakes right above you?"

I looked through the cabinet among the cans of cat food—for Felix? "Do you guys have . . . a cat?"

"No, just Felix."

I stared at Moo. Someone had to tell her. "Moo, Felix is a clock."

"Oh, not *that* Felix. The stray cat who comes by sometimes. I call him Felix." She patted my hand and whispered, "Don't worry, I'm not as bad off as Poppy."

That's when I remembered the Saint John's Wort. It was worth a shot. Maybe it'd take the rust out of the artesian screw.

"Hey, Moo? About Poppy. Have you tried Saint John's Wort?"

Moo stopped stirring the whitish, glue-ish stuff in the pan on the stove. "We're not Catholic, dear."

What? "You don't have to be Catholic."

She went back to stirring. "Well, it's usually Catholics who pray to the saints . . . and sometimes the saint's warts, too, apparently, although that does seem a little strange."

"No, it's not—it's just—"

"But Mike, if you think it'll work, you just tell me how."

"This stuff is an herb that helps with your depression."

"I'm not depressed, dear."

"No, I mean"—I lowered my voice—"you give it to Poppy."

"Oh! I see." She banged the spoon on the side of the pot until the lumps fell off of it. "Okay, where's Junior? We're off to get some warts."

"Past already gave me some. I just wasn't sure if you'd

want it." She seemed kind of sensitive about other things, like failing eyesight and being tired or old.

"Well, of course I do! Poppy needs something. It's not normal to sit in a chair all day like a zombie, Mike."

Poppy made a strangled zombie noise from the other room.

I made Moo call the doctor, like Past said, and she gave Moo the okay. Moo served Poppy his "special recipe" scrapple on a tray in the living room. Then she made us sit down to eat in the kitchen, but fortunately not scrapple.

"Well, I gave it a whirl. Do you think it'll work?" she whispered.

I shook my head. "I hope so. We need it for Misha." It hadn't done anything for Dad as far as I could tell, and I didn't see how a drop or two of some herb could turn a giant vegetable back into a human being. It would take a heck of a lot more than Saint John's Wort. It would take a miracle.

Moo scraped a mouthful of food onto her fork, then put the fork down and looked at her plate. "I know you think it's shellfish, Mike."

I looked down at the lumpy gray-white pile on my plate, too. "Actually, I thought it was tuna." Then I remembered all those cans of cat food in her cabinet and my stomach howled. "It is tuna, isn't it?"

"What? Oh, the casserole? Yes." Moo scraped the tuna blobs around her plate and sighed. "I know you think Poppy is being shellfish."

"*Selfish*. Yeah, I do."

"But he's really not shellfish."

True. I'd put him in the vegetable category, not seafood.

"You haven't warmed to Poppy, have you?"

Warmed? To iceberg lettuce? I shook my head.

Moo sighed. "He's doing the best he can."

"Moo, no offense, but if he were doing his best, he'd be out in the workshop. Don't you think his best is a little lame?"

She patted my hand. "It's hard for you to understand, dear, I know."

Oh, I understood all right. He let everyone else take care of things, handle all the problems, while he just sat there, "away with the fairies." Like Dad. I understood all about that. I was getting so ticked off that I even started wondering about Karen. I mean, everyone was trying to raise money for her, but what was she doing? So I asked Moo.

"Oh, my dear, Karen is zipping all over the countryside on that scooter, getting her adoption papers signed, sealed, and delivered. Goodness, it's a full-time job adopting a child! Well, she may as well get used to it, because that's what having children is all about. Of course, this is rushed because of the adoption deadline. Only four months to get a child, not as leisurely as the other way."

I said, "What other way?" before I realized she was talking about pregnancy.

"Oh, Mike!" Moo's eyes were wide. "Hasn't your father talked to you about sex? Because if not, I can tell you all—"

"No, no—I mean, yes, yes, he has! I know all about that . . . stuff." Dad hadn't told me a thing, but I knew it all from health class, books, and Sasha. And even if I were clueless, I couldn't imagine getting the sex lecture from Moo. My face was hot and felt red just from the mention of it.

I quickly changed the subject to our visit with Dr. P. I asked Moo what he'd meant about Gladys and her family.

"Poor Gladys got a bum rap," Moo said. "Her mother was awful. Taking up with a new man every week. That's no home for a child. And who knows where her father went?" Moo sighed. "So, Gladys keeps everyone at a distance. That's what all those piercings are about. They're her armor. If she rejects everyone first, then no one has a chance to reject her."

"That's dumb. Who would reject her?"

"Well, her father, for one."

I flinched.

"And her mother ignored her, which is as good as rejecting her."

I swallowed hard.

"You know, Mike, being abandoned by your parents can make you feel quite bad about yourself, even though it's not your fault at all."

I shrank in my chair.

"I think the reason she hangs out with Numnut is just to sing in his band."

"He has a band?" Then I remembered the amps, drums, and mikes in his pickup.

"Yes. It's truly awful. But Gladys's father was a singer in some band when he ran off, and that's why I think she likes going to Big Dawg's, so she can play in the band with Numnut."

My toes were wiggling and my brain was firing. "Do you think you could get her to sing on camera? She could do kind of a commercial to raise money for Misha." I could picture the video already: it would begin and end with the bling-framed photo of Misha that sat on Gladys's desk. And a donation request.

"I suppose I could ask her. She might do it for me." Moo stood up and took our dishes to the sink. "Now that you mention it, giving her a way to showcase her singing that doesn't involve Numnut is an excellent idea."

She grinned at me and I gave her a thumbs-up.

Moo went out to the living room to get Poppy's plate. She returned at a trot. "Look! He cleaned his plate!" She pointed at the Saint John's Wort on the counter. "Warts and all!"

I heard a grunt from Poppy's chair that almost sounded like "Hey." A real word.

Moo grinned. "I think it's working already!"

13

ADJACENT ANGLES

—angles that share a common
vertex and edge but do not share
any interior points

The next morning at Past's office, we got to work. Past had gotten the laptop as well as the parts I needed for my Pringles Wi-Fi antenna. I put the antenna together in less than an hour and attached it to the back of his bench. I fired up the laptop and . . . it worked! The signal was great!

"You're brilliant, Mike!" Past said, slapping me on the back.

I guess it wasn't hard to impress a homeless guy.

I have to say, though, that I designed a pretty sweeeeet website. I mean, how could you not love a page that opened with Misha's earnest eyes staring at you? Karen e-mailed me Misha's photos—the one in my Buzz Lightyear shirt and the LEGO one—so I posted them on the Bring Misha Home! website as well as every social networking site I knew, telling the world how they could help bring Misha home. Karen had told me that at first the adoption agency didn't want Misha's photo posted online—something about distant relatives coming forward and claiming him—but she said her faith led her to trust that Misha would end up where he was supposed to, and if by some chance a relative came forward and actually wanted him, maybe that was for the best. I didn't believe her for a minute, but I did believe the next thing she told me: that it rarely, if ever, happens. To be on the safe side, I wasn't giving a last name. Heck, I didn't even know his last name. To us, he was just Misha. Karen's Misha.

"It's looking good," Past said. "How about a tally of the money we're raising?"

"Oh, yeah." Figures I'd forget the part that had to do with numbers. I put counters showing the days left to adopt Misha before the government shut the door—21—and the money Karen still needed—$37,914.62.

I also posted a world map, with Romania on the right side of the screen and Pennsylvania on the left, with all those countries and that huge ocean in between. I started building a LEGO bridge from Romania to Pennsylvania, each block representing $1,000. We had just over two of the forty LEGO bricks that we needed. We were only as far as Croatia. We had a lot of building still to do. But I was determined to complete that bridge.

"I like the LEGO idea, Mike," Past said, "but are you sure blue is a good color? We're about to hit the Adriatic Sea, and there'll be a lot of blue Atlantic Ocean to cover, too."

I looked closely. "The oceans are more turquoise. Blue LEGOs are fine."

Past shrugged. "Okay, I just thought—"

Just then, Karen buzzed up to our bench on her moped, waving a DVD. "It's a video of Misha!"

"Great!" I said. "Can I put it on the Internet?"

Karen beamed. "Of course! But I want to watch it again right now, okay?"

I popped the DVD into the laptop and scooted over next to Past. Karen sat on the other side of me as we watched the screen, waiting.

The image began with a burst of color from bright walls and big windows, and noisy chatter, mostly from women who were bustling around a large room. There were lots of tiny tables with four kids each, sitting quietly.

I adjusted the laptop screen to shield it from the sun and scanned the tables that were in the camera's view, but I couldn't find Misha. "Where is he?"

"Behind that orphanage worker with the white uniform," Karen said.

"All of the women have white uniforms," Past observed as we squinted at the screen.

"The large woman. There." Karen pointed to the left side of the screen.

I craned my head around as if I could peek behind her. "Why doesn't she move?"

"She does," Karen assured me. "Just wait a minute . . . there he is!"

Misha wore a blue plaid flannel shirt and sat at a little table next to two girls, with a bigger boy across from him.

They all looked expectantly at the noisy, chattering women who served plates of steaming food, pasta of some sort.

"They're so quiet," Past said. "The children, I mean."

"And polite," said Karen. "They don't touch their food until everyone is served and they say grace."

The women were babbling away and, of course, I had no idea what they were saying since they spoke Romanian, I assumed. After everyone was served, one of the women picked up a pitcher of milk from a sideboard near Misha and went table by table, filling each kid's plastic cup. A crash off camera stopped her just before she got to Misha's table and she scurried away, stage right.

"Hey, you forgot Misha!" I said.

It was as if he'd heard me! He looked straight at the camera! Pleadingly. Just like in the posters. It was eerie.

Then he looked offscreen where the milk pitcher had disappeared, but the woman didn't return. He raised his hand. You could hear the commotion and several women talking at once, but no one responded to him. Finally, he sighed and put his hand down.

The other three kids at his table stared at their empty cups but did nothing. Misha looked at them, then over at the sideboard where the milk pitchers sat, then off camera where the hustle and bustle was still going on. He stood up and walked over to the sideboard, struggling to lift a full pitcher that seemed half the size of him. The kids at his table looked at each other, wide-eyed. One of the girls giggled and covered her mouth. The bigger boy's eyes kept darting off camera, as if he were the self-appointed lookout.

Misha walked carefully back to the table with the heavy pitcher wobbling in his hands. The three kids stared at him as he slowly lowered the pitcher and, with his hands shaking a little, rested the pitcher on the lip of a tiny plastic cup.

"Hold the cup!" I yelled. "Somebody hold the cup or it's going to—"

Too late. The cup tipped and milk splashed all over the table.

All four kids froze, eyes wide, staring at the wet table. Slowly, Misha put the pitcher down, laid his shirt-sleeves right in the mess, and moved his arms back and forth to soak up the milk. At that point, a piercing male voice made both Past and I jump. It obviously came from right behind the camera, and whatever the cameraman said brought two women over to Misha's table. The video turned to fuzz and static, but not before you heard some shrill chatter that had to mean Misha was being scolded.

"Hey!" I yelled at the screen.

I felt Past's hand on my shoulder. "It's all right, Mike."

"But he was just taking care of things since they weren't," I said.

"The next part is better," Karen promised.

When the video came back into focus, the kids were sitting at the same tables but all the dishes had been cleared away. Misha's wet sleeves were rolled up, but I was relieved to see that he didn't look upset. The women sounded all chipper and in fact started to sing. A piano off camera pounded out a tune I didn't know, but the kids obviously did because they joined in singing, along with clapping and foot stomping in time to the music. I caught Misha smiling a tiny bit at the foot-stomping parts. That would've been my favorite part, too. When it was over, a woman announced something and laughed nervously. The piano started slowly, and just as I was recognizing the tune, although not the woman's words, Karen identified it for us.

"They're teaching the kids 'The Itsy Bitsy Spider.' Watch!"

Sure enough, the kids were being taught the song in English and were trying to follow along. Well, most of them. The other boy at Misha's table was leaning back on his chair, not really paying attention. The two girls were making a pretty good attempt at singing the song and doing the hand movements. Misha was concentrating so hard on the hand movements that he didn't seem to be trying the words. His serious eyes darted between the demonstrator offscreen and his own hands, making the crawling-up-the-water-spout movement, then the rain coming down, then the washing out.

Finally, at the point when I heard the woman's voice say, haltingly, "One—more—time!" Misha went through the finger movements smoothly, and when he held up his thumbs and forefingers to make a big circle for the sun, he broke out into a huge smile! It was the first time I'd really seen him grin, and it was great.

The camera shifted and got his face, perfectly framed inside his little hands. And I heard him say one word when he made that big circle. I swear, I heard him shout it out over everyone else. He said, "Sun!"

14

ZERO PROPERTY

—adding zero to a number leaves
it unchanged

—multiplying a number by
zero results in zero

As far as I could tell, the Saint John's Wort did nothing for Poppy. The deadwood sat in the shop, unmoving, while the unisaw and drill press made nothing but shadows every time I went into the workshop to stare at them. And Poppy still sat in his chair. The rest of us kept at it, though.

On her way to the flea market Thursday morning, Moo dropped me at Karen's house to start my day of filming with a video of Misha's new home. Past didn't come because he refused to get in Tyrone. He was even reluctant for me to get in.

"Stay off the interstate," he cautioned.

"I don't know why he worries so much," Moo grumbled. "Tyrone knows perfectly well how to drive."

We got to Karen's without any mishaps. Her house was straight out of a fairy-tale book, a brick Cape Cod with one of those wooden gnome doors, the kind that's rounded at the top. The inside was fairy tale-ish, too, and I saw every inch of it, including the kitchen sink, table, and fridge, because Karen made me film everything.

"Don't forget Mr. Bubble," she said in the bathroom. "Oh, and here's his Superman toothbrush!"

In the bedroom I had to film each drawer of his dresser, including his "big boy" underwear, then his soccer bedspread, the toy chest, and the bookcase full of books. When she started reading each one out loud, I finally had to stop her. She looked surprised.

"Can we limit it to just the books on the top shelf?" I asked.

It was definitely a video that would need heavy editing.

But Karen's pride and joy was in the little fenced backyard: a sandbox. And it was amazing: two tiers with a ramp from the upper-level box down to the larger bottom box. It had every kind of backhoe, front-end loader, and truck that any kid could want.

"I got them all from the flea market for under five dollars," Karen explained.

"Not the sandbox, though," I said. "You can't buy something like this. It's priceless."

The normally bubbly Karen stood very still. "You're right, Mike. It is priceless. My husband built it. He wanted to leave something for Misha."

Whoa. "He knew about Misha?"

She nodded. "We got a DVD just before he died." She

blinked and sniffled a few times. "I know he'd be so happy for me, and Misha. Now we have each other."

My knees practically buckled under me. If we failed . . . well, we wouldn't fail. It just wasn't an option.

I was only half paying attention when I was back at Moo's, recording the promotional video for her vinegars for sale, although I tuned in as she explained her three-bottles-of-vinegar plan. Who needed that many bottles of vinegar—per week?

Next, she drove me to the bank. "You need to work on Gladys," Moo explained. "I've tried to convince her to play guitar and sing for your video, but she's so shy. I asked Past to meet you there."

The air-conditioning was blasting when Past and I entered the bank, and it felt great.

"Hi, Gladys." I sat down next to Past on one of the chairs in front of her desk.

Past folded his arms and I noticed he wore a new blue button-down shirt.

"So," I said, "how about singing for us, Gladys?"

She pulled the monitor in front of her face.

I leaned over and tilted her monitor so she couldn't hide behind it. "Come on, you have a great voice."

"How do you know?" Her face was pink except for a white circle around her cheek stud.

"Everyone says so. I heard you used to sing in church."

"That was a long time ago. And I don't like to sing in front of a crowd."

"You sing in a band," Past said slowly. "How is that not singing in front of a crowd?"

"It's a dive bar. It's dark!" Gladys said. "No one's listening, anyway. They're talking and laughing and drinking. They hardly notice me. Mostly they just hear my guitar."

She pulled the monitor back to its original position and clicked her computer keys a mile a minute.

Past's Bono eyes blinked and looked thoughtfully at Gladys.

But I wasn't cutting anyone any slack, not when Misha was at stake. "Come on, Gladys—"

"By the way, Mike," she interrupted me, "your dad hasn't sent that deposit yet."

I practically jumped out of my chair. "What! He's such an idiot!"

"I thought he was a genius," said Past.

"Not when it comes to real life. Hey, can I send him a message?" I reached over her desk before she even answered, bumping her arm.

"Are you putting moves on my woman?" a slow, monotone voice behind me asked.

My woman? Was he serious? I swung around to see a short hairy dude in a black skull T-shirt. His dark hair practically covered his face except for a narrow opening where it looked like he was peeking out from behind an almost closed door.

I heard Gladys's voice. "It's okay, babe."

Babe? Was *she* serious?

"This is Mike and this is Past," Gladys said, pointing to us.

"I'm Numchuck," the guy said in his gravelly monotone.

"I see," said Past. "Is that your name or your occupation?"

"Huh?" Numchuck looked stunned as he peered out from behind his hair, like a door had been slammed in his face.

I swear, *I'm embarrassed* was practically written on Gladys's face.

"I'm running on empty," Numchuck said to Gladys.

"I can tell," Past said.

"What?" he growled.

"Oh, I'm sorry—did you mean you're hungry? The soup kitchen opens shortly." Past looked at the dude and smiled. "I'd be happy to tell you where to go."

"It's my truck that's empty. Needs gas," Numchuck said.

Gladys yanked her bag out of a desk drawer and took out a wad of bills.

Numchuck took the cash and turned to go.

Past reached out and grabbed his arm. "Thank you, Gladys," he said pointedly, "for giving me money."

Numchuck spun around to face Gladys, immediately grabbing Past in a headlock. "What'd you give him money for?"

"Hey, let him go!" I yelled.

From under Numchuck's arm, Past managed to say, "I was merely indicating that it would be polite for you to thank her for the money."

Numchuck released him, sniffing the air. "That's some weird deodorant you've got."

Past immediately dropped his arms, then crossed them against his chest, making a quick exit. I followed.

Outside the bank, I had to push Past's cart because he refused to expose his armpits, requiring him to keep his arms clasped across his chest like they were his armor.

"He's a drug-head, Past. Just ignore what he said."

"Well, I am a little . . . odiferous."

I shrugged, not wanting to admit that Numnut might have had a point. "If you're concerned about it, do they have showers at the soup kitchen?"

"I did take a shower when I put on this shirt and I thought I was smelling . . . fresh."

"Don't worry about it." I debated telling him that eBay required clean shirts so I'd have to wash this one, too.

"No, I think it's a good wake-up call. I'm thankful, actually."

I sneered. "I'm not!"

"We can learn from all types, my friend. Speaking of which, don't you need to contact your father about the money? And his diet?"

I hit a bump in the sidewalk and shoved the cart hard to get past it. The wheels spun wildly and the cart fish-tailed until I grabbed it and got it back on track. I wished I could get that much reaction out of Dad. "Yeah, I'll contact him. But he's such an idiot."

Past reached out his hand and grabbed the cart, stopping it. He quickly resumed his arms-as-armor position.

"What?" I sounded as annoyed as I felt. His eyes were so sad and serious that I wished I hadn't sounded harsh. "What?" I said again, more gently this time.

Past's Bono eyes looked at me. "You never know when you'll lose someone."

I sighed and started pushing the cart again. "I only lose him in the grocery store because he can't remember where anything is, even though we've been going to the same store for ten years. I can't lose him in Romania. He has a handler." I thought of Ferdi. "He'll put him on a plane—after making the reservation for him and getting his ticket—and send him back to D.C. in a month."

"Even so," he said quietly, "it would be good to keep up contact. And not just for the money. You have news."

I thought, uncomfortably, of the nonexistent artesian screw and the math worksheets I hadn't even looked at.

"You're playing an important role in saving a young soul."

I snorted.

"Fortunately, you have an able assistant."

I didn't mention that my able assistant had his arms plastered against his chest, making them useless, so I was pushing his shopping cart of assorted odd items for him.

"The poor boy has a parent who can't take care of him."

I stopped the cart. "Who are you talking about?"

"Misha."

"He's an orphan. He doesn't have parents."

Past shook his head. "It's not uncommon, I'm afraid.

Children are given up for adoption because the parent—sometimes both parents—are unable to care for them properly."

"Unable to care for him properly?" I thought of Dad. And me. "Since when do kids get adopted because of lousy parenting?"

"It's more common that you'd think. It's also a matter of money. Often there's not enough money to take care of a child."

"Oh, come on. How can you be so poor that you can't even take care of your own kid?"

Past stared at me, and then I realized, *How could I be so stupid that I'd ask a homeless guy a question like that?*

I swallowed hard. "I'll IM Dad when we get back to your office." And I did. Creatively.

Hi, Dad. 'Sup?

Excuse me?

Nothing. I was wondering what's happening with the money.

What is happening with the artesian screw project? I hope you're recording the developments. What has Poppy taught you thus far?

Poppy? I guess I'd have to say patience.

I typed fast, before he thought of any more questions.

People are focused on a really important project in town.

What is that?

I started typing but stopped. He wouldn't get it. Making YouTube videos to help adopt an orphan? I could say I was working with a teacher because Karen really was a teacher, but then he'd want to know what exactly I was working on. And he wouldn't be impressed if I said I was working with a minister, either, whatever denomination Karen was. Unless . . .

It's a special project for a minister of education in PA.

That sounded impressive!

What is the project concerning exactly?

It's kind of hard to explain. It's sort of a population study.

Whoa! I was pretty good at this!

That's a soft "social science" and of less value than real science.

Yeah. Because why would we want to learn about anything *social*? That had to do with people. And life. It's so much better to stick with numbers.

Dad just didn't get it. Had he always been like this? I thought of the Saint John's Wort on our kitchen counter. Did he act this way because he was depressed? And he used to be normal? Or was he always this way and that's what was making him depressed?

Now, tell me about the artesian screw.

Dad! You forgot to send money to Moo's account.

Was I supposed to? I don't recall that.

Yes, Dad. Do I need to go into all the descriptions again about how poor they are?

I'll have Ferdi take care of it. In the meantime, you should spend less effort on the population study than on the en-

gineering project, which has much more value. You need
to learn skills so you don't end up on the street.

I gritted my teeth and snapped Past's laptop shut.

Past jerked up from rummaging in his shopping cart.
"So? What did he say?"

I looked at him, the guy who'd ended up on the street,
and shook my head. "Absolutely nothing of value."

15

DIFFERENCE

—how much one number differs from another

Somehow I made it back to Moo's. I was so mad at Dad that I'm not even sure how I got there. I mean, he hadn't seen me in a week and he never even checked to see if I'd gotten here—it was only because I IM'ed him that he knew. And I told him how badly we needed money, and he forgot! Like I was worthless. Then when I sent him a message telling him what I was doing, making it sound even better than it was, he still blew me off. It still wasn't good enough. All he cared about was Poppy's engineering project that didn't even exist! And Poppy wouldn't work on the real project, making boxes, even though he knew how critical his role was in getting Misha adopted. He just sat there like a lump!

When I swung the front door open, Moo was struggling toward me with a huge garbage bag almost as big as she was.

"Moo! What are you doing?"

She put it down, panting, her face red. "It's Thursday."

"What?"

"Trash day tomorrow."

I looked at Poppy, who had the yellow yardstick across his lap. "Moo, you shouldn't be the one doing this." I was seething, my voice loud so it could penetrate Poppy's stupor.

He didn't even flinch. It was as easy to get through to Poppy as it was to Dad.

I gritted my teeth. "I'll handle it."

"Thank you so much, Mike. I need to finish some paperwork." She told me where the trash can was and headed to the kitchen.

I glared at Poppy and hissed, "You should be doing this and you know it!"

When I joined Moo in the kitchen—after I'd taken care of the trash and given Poppy another dirty look about it— she was squinting at some forms on the table, her nose about two inches from the paper.

"What are you reading?"

"I made a bargain with Gladys. I told her I'd fill out these direct deposit forms for our Social Security checks if she'd sing for you on YouTube."

I sat down heavily. "Direct deposit is a good idea, Moo. You'll be happy you did it."

She looked up at me ruefully. "All I said was I'd fill them out. I never said I'd hand them in."

"Moo!"

"Oh, all right, I suppose it's safe. But"—she tapped her pen on the form several times—"who can even read these words? They've made them so tiny."

"Here," I said, gently pulling the pen out of her hand and pulling the forms toward me. "I'll do it."

"I've started you off with my name and Poppy's," she said proudly.

First, I noticed how shaky and oversized her handwriting was. Second, I saw their real names. Beulah Wealthea O'Brien and Heinrich Gunther O'Brien. Whoa, no wonder they went with Moo and Poppy. Third, I realized that Moo had written her name on the line for "Name of Financial Institution" and Poppy's on the "Account Number" line. I asked her for her checkbook to get her account number and went to work.

"All you'll need to do is sign the form when I'm done. And get"—I jerked my thumb toward the living room—"to sign it, and you'll be all set."

"Thank you, dear!"

I barely got started filling in the blanks when the tapping started. I ignored it at first, but it got louder. I looked at Moo, cooking scrapple at the stove, but realized the noise was coming from behind me. And it was getting more irritating every second. "What *is* that?"

"What, dear?"

"That tapping sound!"

Her shoulders drooped. "I'm late with supper. I think Poppy's getting impatient."

I felt my grip tighten on the pen and the words on the form grow hazy as my eyes narrowed. The tapping continued.

"Oh! I need to grab a couple of tomatoes from the garden. Past says they have lycopene and would be good for Poppy, so I'm going to try mixing them in with his scrapple."

As soon as she went out the back door, I stood up to yell at Poppy through the pass-through. I was just in time to see him push the hands of the Felix clock with the yardstick. The clock now read nine fifteen. So that's how the clock kept changing! Poppy started tapping on Felix, loudly, demanding his dinner. All I could think was, *How dare he!*

That's when I lost it.

I marched into the living room, grabbed the yardstick out of Poppy's hand, and broke it in two. His eyes grew wide and they locked on mine for a moment before his lips stuck out in a defiant pout and he stared back at Felix. I looked at the two pieces of yardstick, surprised I'd even done that, and dropped them. When I looked at Poppy, I saw that his face was red and his nostrils were flared, but one of his hair horns had flopped over. He was still staring up at the Felix clock.

"Yeah," I said. "It's time, all right. It's time for you to move your butt!"

He was breathing heavily, but other than his chest rising and falling, he didn't budge. He wouldn't even look at me.

"And you know what else?" I added. "I'm going out to the workshop. *Your* workshop. And I'm going to use *your* tools to make all those boxes that *you're* supposed to be out there making!"

His grunt came out sounding more like a yelp, but that didn't stop me. I grabbed the key from the row of hooks by the door and stormed out to the workshop.

16

REGROUP

—rearrange the formation of a group of numbers

I t's not a good idea to go into a workshop when you're angry, especially when you're not all that good at woodworking. I couldn't even cut one straight piece, never mind six pieces that could actually be made into a box. Nothing fit together no matter how many times I ran it through another pass on the radial arm saw. And forget cutting angles to get pieces to wedge together. You need math to do woodworking, so that's why I'm not too good at it. In the end, I was left with about a million assorted sizes of excellent quality toothpicks.

I looked up at the sheet of white lined notebook paper taped above the door. It was Moo's shaky writing but big enough to read easily. *What would Oprah say?* I wasn't sure what words Oprah would use to describe my mess, but I let out a whole slew of words until the door opened and Moo walked in.

She saw the splinters of wood all over the floor and

table saw and almost dropped the plate of cookies she was holding. She kept looking behind her at the door like she was worried Poppy might come in and see what I'd done. As if.

"Oh, dear," she said, her knuckles growing white as she gripped the plate.

"Yeah. I messed up. Big-time."

"You just need more experience." She sighed. "I wish Poppy would teach you. He's very good at woodworking, you know."

Something inside me snapped. Again. Like the yardstick. "No, I don't know," I yelled, "because he won't get his butt out of that stupid chair!"

She took a step back and put the plate on top of the scraps of wood covering the workbench. "It's frustrating, isn't it? But we all handle things differently." She bent down and picked up a couple of nails under the workbench that I guess I'd missed when I cleaned up the shop. She walked over to the table saw, dropped them in the cardboard box labeled OLD NAILS, and smiled. "Some of us are more extreme cases than others."

I wiped the sweat from my upper lip and nodded. Yeah, and why did they all have to end up in my life? I stared at her for a moment, with her hand on the box of nails, still smiling. I had to ask her. "How did you handle my dad? I mean, what was he like as a kid?"

"Let's go inside and I'll tell you a little about him."

I grabbed the cookies from the workbench and followed her to the kitchen. I remembered her last cookie disaster, but this time the kitchen had a warm chocolate smell that tempted me, and I dug in. "Whoa, these are delicious."

"I've just finished the chocolate chip and I'm moving on to snickerdoodles. They're doing a fund-raiser a few towns away for Misha's adoption. Isn't that nice?"

I nodded, my mouth full of cookies.

Moo cracked an egg into a bowl on the counter. "Mike, I must say, your dad was a child who was away with the fairies if there ever was one."

"Spacey, right?"

"He was positively in orbit, dear."

"He's a genius." I didn't say it with affection.

She pressed her lips together and looked at me, then eyed the doorway between the kitchen and living room.

"What?" I asked.

"He clipped his shoulder on that door frame every time he walked through it."

I shrugged. "He never looks where he's going."

"Sometimes he would wear two different shoes."

"I know."

"He never played with the other children even though there were a lot in the neighborhood back then."

So, he'd always been different. It must be part of being a genius.

Moo whisked the contents of the bowl. "And the fire department had to come twice."

"What?"

"THE FIRE DEPARTMENT HAD TO—"

"Yes, but why? He started two fires?"

"No, just one. The other time he was on the roof and couldn't get down."

"What happened?"

"Let's see. He was on the roof because he was measuring angles or something . . . I'm not even sure, but he panicked once he looked down, and neither Poppy nor I could get him to budge."

"And the fire?"

She reached for the glass canister of flour on the counter and pulled it forward, revealing a black patch on the pink countertop. "Your dad said it was a science experiment."

I stared at the cracked, bubbly blackness against the pink swirls of countertop. "Weren't you mad at him?"

"Well . . ." She took my hand and pulled me over to the kitchen table, where we both sat down. "He obviously has some problems, dear."

"Problems? He's a genius."

"I know, dear," she said sadly, as if it were some terrible disease.

"Moo . . . he's lucky."

She squinted at me for a moment, then smiled and patted my hand. "Yes, dear, because he has you." She looked through the pass-through at Poppy.

Suddenly, a woman's voice sang loudly from somewhere in the kitchen.

Let's get physical!

Moo jumped. "That's my song!" Her yellow sneakers ran over to Junior at the edge of the counter and she dug around inside while the song continued.

Moo flipped the phone open, peering sideways at it as she held it away from her head. "Yes?" she said loudly. "Oh, hello, Karen! I'm making the cookies right now. I finished the chocolate chip and—" She paused, her brow furrowing. "Slow down, dear. Take a deep breath." Moo nodded, chewing on her lips. "Oh, I'm so sorry. Yes, of course, dear, you need to go. . . . Who? Gladys? Oh, dear." Moo's eyes darted to the kitchen window and she peered out back into the darkness. "Uh-huh, and you talked with Past?"

Gladys? Past? What was she talking about?

"Well, of course we're going to help you, Karen! We all want Misha home. Everything will be fine. You take care now. Bye-bye."

"What's up?" I asked as she closed her phone and dropped it back in Junior.

"Oh, dear. Poor Karen. Her father had a stroke, so she has to go to Ohio and take care of him and her mother. She's all upset about that, and about leaving town when everyone's trying to help her." Moo pulled on her hoodie strings. "I hope everything still works out all right with Misha."

I almost gagged on my cookie, and clutched the edge of the table. "Misha? Why wouldn't it work out?"

"Karen's the organizer and I'm not sure how well the rest of us will do without her. She already called Past, who said he'd do what he could do, but . . ." She waved her hand. "And then there's poor Gladys."

I was still reeling from the idea of Misha not getting adopted. "What about Gladys?"

"Karen says she's very upset. Gladys is sensitive about . . . family issues because of her own. It's as if she put all her hopes for a family into helping Misha and Karen make one." Moo still clutched her hoodie strings and stared out the kitchen window. "When she's upset, she likes to go down to the lake and think. She always sits in a spot near our house. I wonder if she's there now. . . . Of course, I can't leave my cookies in the oven or they'll burn. Poor Gladys."

I stood up. "I can go and see if she's there."

"Oh, would you, Mike?"

"Sure. Um, what do you want me to say?"

She patted my arm. "You'll think of something, dear, I'm sure."

It took a few minutes for my eyes to adjust to the darkness outside, which was my excuse for why I tripped twice walking down the hill toward the lake. It wasn't because I was nervous. Really.

I heard the rippling of water and the splashing plops of fish or frogs before I actually saw Gladys. She was sitting in a little heap on the shore near a scrubby bush. I didn't want to scare her by walking right up to her and surprising her, so I called out, "Hi. It's me, Mike."

Gladys turned and nodded. "Hi," she said softly.

I walked over and sat on the pebbly ground next to her. "Moo told me about Karen."

She looked out at the lake for a while before picking up a stone and throwing it in. "I knew it would never work."

"What?"

"Adoption. It sounds good. It doesn't happen like it does in movies, though."

"Hey, my best friend was adopted from Russia. It happens. I've seen it."

"Maybe in other places or for other people. Not here."

"Why not?"

She gazed across Lake Revival, looking small and not at all tough, now that you couldn't see all the piercings and tattoos. She rocked gently. "We're a bunch of misfits, not families. I mean, look at the name of our town. Do Over. We can't get it right."

"Not the first time, maybe, but there's always a second chance."

"At having a family?" She said it with such scorn, it was like she knew what failures Dad and I were at being a family.

"Sure," I said, but my voice didn't sound at all convincing.

She threw in another stone. "This whole project is sunk."

"Don't say that! It is not!"

"Look, you're sweet, but you don't know anything about—"

"I don't know anything about what?" I stared at her, my eyes narrowed. "I don't know anything about family? About little boys? Who don't have moms? About . . . Misha?" I threw my own stone into the lake. Hard. "What's there to know, huh? Misha needs a home. Karen wants him. That's all there is. It's simple. And no one's going to stop it."

She sighed. "There's no artisan's crew to make the money—"

"We're making money! We're selling stuff. We're almost up to five thousand now."

"And we need forty. Now Karen's gone and there's no one to lead the project."

"There are people around."

She stared at me. "Like who?"

I started to suggest Moo but stopped. She wasn't the most organized person. Past? I didn't think Gladys would accept a homeless guy as leader, even though he didn't seem like your typical homeless guy. "How about the guys at the park who make porch pals?"

"Oh, come on. Haven't you heard their nickname? 'The three stooges.' You want to put them in charge?"

Gladys wasn't helping the situation. But maybe she should. "What about you?"

"Me?" She wrapped her arms around herself and looked away. "Let's just say I'm not exactly an expert on building families."

"Who is?" I asked.

"Probably anyone but me," she said, her voice shaky.

When she started sniffling, I almost croaked. I hadn't meant to make her cry. Oh, man, now I'd done it. I was supposed to be making her feel better! The words were out of my mouth before my brain had a chance to check them out. "I'll handle it. I mean, if everyone's okay with that."

What was I saying? Did I think this was some computer quest game, *Save the Orphan*, where I was playing the role of Dumb Kid: practically an orphan in his own home; knows ex-orphan who now has a happy family. Situation: hopeless. Likelihood of Success—

"Really?" she asked softly. "You'd do that?" Her eyes turned to me and her blinking slowed down.

Maybe if she'd laughed, I would've laughed, too, and it would've all been over. But she didn't. She looked at me . . . not like I was a dumb kid, but a guy . . . a guy who was pretty cool, capable, even clever. A guy who could actually save Misha and bring him home. "Yeah," I heard myself say. "Don't worry. It'll happen. I'll make it happen."

She stared at me with big, dark, glistening eyes. I felt like we were moving closer and closer to each other. My heart started beating fast and my breathing sped up so much, I tried hard to keep from panting. Was this going to be a kiss? My first real kiss? Was this how it happened? It was like watching a YouTube, except I was in it.

"Snicker-DOOOO-dles!" Moo's voice rang out from the house. "Gladys! Mike! Come get some SNICKERDOODLES!"

The YouTube screeched to a halt. Gladys and I looked at each other and smiled, then grinned, then outright laughed.

17

PROBLEM

—a question where math is used
to figure out the answer

I wasn't laughing the next morning. Everyone—Karen, Gladys, Moo, Past—said I should be the one. The leader. The big boss. The head honcho. Now a kid's life was in my hands. I stared at the photo of Misha with his LEGO bridge. I'd set the picture Karen gave me on my nightstand with my own blue LEGO brick weighing it down. I didn't want it to fall or fly away in the breeze from the fan. It was such a huge commitment. Like I was bringing this kid home all by myself. How was I going to do that? I mean, sure, others would help, but the bottom line was, it was up to me. I was responsible for this kid's life. If I didn't do my job . . . well, it wouldn't get done.

I shivered on my bed, even though it was already a hot day. It made me freeze to think of things like all the unfinished paperwork in Karen's adoption file. She called her file of papers a "dossier." I felt like some kind of James Bond who had to secure the secret file or someone's life would be . . . over. Except that, unlike Bond, I had no idea what to do and no Q with a lab of tools to help me. Also, I'm pretty sure James Bond didn't have dyscalculia to mix him up. I never heard him call himself agent Seven-Double-O instead of Double-O-Seven.

I asked Moo to drop me at Past's office while she made a scrapple run. I paced in front of his bench while he followed my movements like he was watching a tennis match, nodding at every point I made.

"So, Poppy's not making the boxes and it doesn't look like he's going to. No one else can make them without his help. I tried but that was a total joke. Moo wants to bake stuff and sell it but we don't have that much money for ingredients. She can still do the vinegar because it's cheap and she grows the herbs herself, but are those really going to sell? Gladys is knitting bling but refusing to sing, even though Moo says that's what Gladys really wants to do with her life. Porch pal production, at least, is going well."

Past smiled and gave two thumbs-up.

"But we still need almost thirty-five thousand dollars. The LEGO bridge is barely past Italy, not even at the Atlantic Ocean yet. And there's only fifteen days left until the deadline. Wait!" I stopped pacing. "Does she need all forty thousand by then? Because she can't buy her ticket until she knows when she's supposed to go to Romania. Maybe we don't need to raise it all."

"Actually," said Past, "you can buy an open ticket, and she needs to show the adoption agency that she has all the necessary funds by the July fifteenth date."

I started pacing again. "We also need to finish the dossier of adoption papers. If something goes wrong with the paperwork, it'll ruin everything! Will people even listen to me if I call the embassy or immigration service or adoption agency? Do you think my voice is deep enough? Do I sound like an adult?"

"Whoa, Mike, I—"

"Karen said we could pay a service to do it but that costs a lot of money. But maybe it's worth it. There are numbers involved and I could totally screw that up!"

Past looked at me, almost hurt. "Mike. Aren't you forgetting something?"

"What?"

"You can always ask someone for help."

I threw my arms in the air. "Who?"

"Me."

I let my arms drop and didn't say anything.

"Yes, me," he repeated, scowling.

"Okay," I said. Why not? At least he was an adult and people might listen to him. Over the phone, no one would know he was homeless. Plus, he didn't have math disabilities, as far as I knew. "We need to figure out what paperwork has to be done. I don't know the first thing about adoptions."

"Before she left last night, Karen brought her laptop and files to me, so—"

"You?"

"Is something wrong with that?"

"No," I said quickly, although I didn't state the obvious. *You're homeless, dude.* "Um, it's just that you don't have a great storage place for them."

"What do you think the plastic bags are for?"

He pulled his cart around and uncovered it, showing me the large box of files as well as a laptop. "Let's get to work."

We used Karen's computer, jiggled the Pringles can for Wi-Fi access, and brought up the adoption agency's site that gave all the steps to organize a dossier. We found a checklist and went through the box of files Karen left, checking off what she had already and figuring out what she still needed.

"She's got her criminal background check, but she still needs to get fingerprinted," Past said. "It looks like that can be done at any police station, so we need to call her and remind her to go do that while she's with her parents. It's a good thing she already did her home inspection and had all her visits with the social worker. But someone should take these documents to Harrisburg to get the Apostilles."

It was like he was speaking a foreign language. "What?"

"The documents need special seals, and the courthouse at the state capital is the only place it can be done. I'd rather they be delivered than use the mail and hope the right office knows what to do with them. If they got lost, it'd be months before we'd get new ones."

"We can't afford months!"

"I know. I'll figure out how to take care of that.

Meanwhile"—Past held up a thin file—"she seems to only have two letters of reference. She needs three."

"Great. Who are we going to get to do that?"

"I'll write one."

I tried to think of a tactful way to say it. "Dude. Are you sure that's a good idea?"

He raised his eyebrows.

"I mean . . . what are you going to put as your address?"

"I have an address." He leaned forward and looked down the street, as if searching for an imaginary house. "I'll type it up on her laptop." He started typing immediately.

"Maybe we can print it out at the bank," I said, trying to see what he'd typed. "We need to go see Gladys anyway, to hand in Moo's direct deposit form." And maybe Gladys could come up with someone other than a homeless person to write the letter of recommendation.

"Hi, Me-Mike!" Guido called.

He and the other stooges sat down at the nearby bench with cups of coffee and a newspaper.

"We hear you're in charge." Jerry grinned at me.

"How did you hear?"

Guido laughed and nudged Jerry. "He still thinks he's in the big city. He doesn't know we all know each other's business."

I read Past's letter over his shoulder as he typed. It sounded pretty darn good. So did his letterhead.

"I borrowed your job title," Past said.

I laughed. "Community organizer? I'm not a community organizer!"

He smirked. "I think you are."

"Good thing, too," Guido said, lowering his newspaper to look over at us. "Do Over Day is a week from tomorrow."

Past stopped typing and looked at me. "I forgot about that. Who's going to take care of it?"

"Why are you looking at me? I don't even know what you guys are talking about."

Guido rolled his eyes at Jerry and Spud. "Do Over Day. You know, we have it every year."

"Hey, I'm working on getting Misha adopted. Someone else can take care of Do Over Day, whatever that is."

"The whole point of Do Over Day," said Jerry, "is to make money for a good cause. Guess what the good cause is this year?"

"How should I know?"

"Getting Misha adopted! That's why Karen was running it."

"What? Wait a minute. You mean I'm supposed to run Do Over Day, too?"

"Well," said Guido, "you're the new Karen."

"I am not! I don't know how to do this! Maybe we should skip Do Over Day this year."

The three stooges stared at each other and then me.

Guido cleared his throat. "You're going to skip making money for Misha?"

"Well . . . how much money do you usually get?"

"Several thousand. And it'll be more this year because it's not just some charity. It's for someone we know. It's for Misha."

I sighed. "Okay. But I have no clue what I'm doing."

"You'll figure it out, though, I'm sure. You seem like a bright kid."

"No, I'm not. Seriously."

"Don't worry, Mike," said Past. "I'll help you. I can lead the chorus."

"Chorus? What chorus?"

"The one you put together," Guido said from behind his paper.

"Are you kidding me? I can't—I—I wouldn't even know where to start!"

"You'll need a theme song—something international, since the kid is from Romania," Guido said, looking at the others.

All three stooges started singing some song I didn't recognize.

"Hey!" Past shouted over to them.

The three stooges stopped.

Past folded his arms. "I don't think the theme song from *The Love Boat* counts, even if it's cruising international waters." He looked at me, with some desperation. "Mike? Any ideas?"

"Other than this is completely crazy?"

"He means a song, Mike," Jerry said.

"I know that!" I took a deep breath. A song for an international kid? I immediately thought of the song my fourth-grade class did for United Nations Day. We even got on TV. Sasha did a solo because the song had foreign languages. It was hard for him to sing, though, because he and I kept giggling. His parents were sitting in the front row, grinning like crazy, especially his dad—

"Are you with us, Mike?" It was Past.

"What? Oh. Yeah."

Guido slapped his paper down. "Does that mean you've come up with a song?"

I nodded. "As a matter of fact, I have a good one." I looked at Past. "How am I going to organize all this? I can't—"

Past's phone rang and he picked it up. "Yes?" His eyes widened as he looked at me. "You're with which paper? *The Daily American*? Yes, I know Karen. . . . Uh-huh."

He nodded as he listened.

"Oh, I agree. It makes an excellent human interest story. This boy is driven to get the kid adopted." He nodded. "Right, Michael. What? No, that's the teenager. The Romanian orphan's name is Misha, which also means Michael, by the way." Past sighed and gave a faint smile. "More than a coincidence? I've heard that from others."

"See!" Jerry shouted.

Past waved his hand at Jerry as he pushed the phone up against his ear. "Sure, you could call it fate. Uh-huh, *kismet* works, too." He rolled his eyes, then winked at me. "*Miracle* might be a little strong, but why not?"

"What did we tell you?" Guido said.

"Yes, he's in charge of Do Over Day, too. Uh-huh. Just a minute." He looked at me. "How old are you, Mike?"

"Fourteen."

He spoke into the phone. "Fourteen. Yes, just call

whenever you're ready to do the interview." He shut the phone. "We have the power of the press behind us now, Mike. You're going to be in the paper."

I let that sink in as we walked to the bank. A newspaper? I wasn't sure how I felt about it, but at least it was free advertising. Now I just had to figure out what to advertise about Do Over Day. I grilled Past on what it really needed—or what I really needed to do to make it happen.

We figured I could enlist moms like Tresa and her friends to organize the kid games, Moo and her friends to make baked goods, Gladys to handle the money part of it, and Past said he'd lead the chorus once I got all the singers.

"How am I going to find singers for a whole chorus?"

"I'll help you round up the usual suspects," Past assured me.

"Fine. I'll make up some flyers." That's how I'd use the math worksheets Dad sent. The blank side would now have Do Over Day information and photos of Misha. Like Moo had predicted, I was going to do something very special with that scrap paper. "I'll also advertise it on Facebook and YouTube. How big a crowd can we handle?"

"Do you seriously think that many people will come?" Past seemed doubtful.

"It's possible. We need to get Shop 'n Save to donate the food, so I better go talk with the manager there. Hey! Maybe we can get cotton candy and funnel cake concessions."

Past stopped, a look of horror on his face. "Please. Let me take care of the food. I want to ensure that we're offering healthy choices."

I shrugged. "As long as we've got food and live music, we can call it a fair. And a moon bounce. Kids will drag their parents in if they see one of those."

"We usually just have three-legged races, sack races, egg races, that kind of thing. It's cheaper so the profit margin is higher."

"Okay, I'll have people bring their own sacks because we might run out."

Past chuckled. "You really think a lot of people are going to come, don't you?"

"Absolutely! By the time I'm done advertising, we could have thousands."

Past stopped chuckling and eyed me. "You may be right. Okay, I'm going to enlist help from some of the guys."

"What guys?"

"The soup kitchen."

I looked at him.

"Hey, just because they're homeless doesn't mean they're not capable. A lot of them work but don't have enough money"—he started blinking rapidly—"or for whatever reason, they don't have a home."

"Are any of them good with power tools? I mean, could they make Poppy's boxes?"

"I don't know about that. But I'm sure they can help run the games, direct the parking, serve food, things like that. It's held right here in the park."

"What if it rains?"

"We use the soup kitchen since it's right next to the park."

145

I started some new lists of all the things I had to do for Do Over Day, and another list of the points I should make with that reporter. As soon as we had a newspaper article, I'd send the link to my teachers, friends, anyone I could think of to spread the word, even my neighbors. Whatever my school was selling, I could always get some neighbors to buy it. And it was a lot easier to sell this cause—*Build a Family, Adopt a Child*—than magazines or wrapping paper.

Past and I checked the street outside the bank. No Numnut or F-350 pickup. It was safe to go in.

I handed Gladys Moo's direct deposit forms. "Completed and signed. Now you have to sing on camera."

Gladys, who'd started to smile, stopped. "Look, guys, I really—"

"A deal's a deal." I picked up the bling-framed photo of Misha and held it in front of her. I also used my earnest Misha eyes to add to the appeal.

"Fine," she said, in a voice of defeat, "but is anyone going to be there while you're filming?"

"We'll use the soup kitchen, after it's closed," Past assured her.

"You know," I said casually, "it'd be really great if you could sing at Do Over Day—"

Gladys went totally pale and shook her head. "I—I can play the guitar for you."

"Yeah, but could you also sing?" I asked.

"One step at a time," Past murmured.

His phone rang and he stood up. "Excuse us, that's the press."

We ducked out of the bank as Past answered. It was actually Karen calling from Ohio, checking on how things were going. We went back inside to ask Gladys about donations to the cause. We were several thousand up from the previous week!

Past and I gave each other a high five as he relayed the news to Karen.

Gladys smiled. "Just wait until the eBay sales come in!"

But the real success of the day was the porch pals video. I decided a kid story was appropriate. As a play. "Goldilocks and the Three Bears." I even got Past to act it out with the three stooges. They each rubber-banded the arms and legs of a porch pal to their own arms and legs. When they moved, it looked like live porch pals. Sure, you could tell that there was a person attached to the back of the big stuffed porch pal, but that made it even funnier, especially since Spud's bald head peeked out above the blond yarn of the Goldilocks doll. Guido did a great job as Baby Bear and Past was a very dignified Papa Bear, but Jerry's swishy, sexy Mama Bear about killed me.

I posted it on our website, all the networking sites, as well as YouTube. By the next day, we already had a lot of hits and an average four-star rating, so if anyone read the appeal at the end of the video, we ought to get some donations.

Misha was coming home!

18

SLIDE

—movement of a figure along a line

There's a difference between watching videos and actually donating money, though. People must've been too busy rolling on the floor laughing to see our appeal for cash at the end. I kept thinking about how much more money we'd raise if Poppy would just get off his butt and make those boxes.

"How's Poppy doing?" said Past as we entered the quiet soup kitchen to set up for Gladys. "Any movement?"

I slumped on a chair at one of the long tables inside, exhausted from days of preparing for Do Over Day—printing and posting flyers, getting the word out electronically, talking to just about everyone in town about what they needed to do. "Poppy? Yeah, he's moving, all right. Now he's putting his duck slippers all around the house to give us hints of what he wants. First, Moo found one under the sink where he keeps his Preparation H, because he was almost out. Then she found one in the fridge where she normally puts his soda, but she'd run out. And last night he wanted his A.1. sauce for his scrapple, only I didn't know that, and Moo was out talking to her tomatoes, so no matter how many times he smacked his busted yardstick on Felix—"

Past flinched.

"—Felix the clock—I didn't get him what he wanted, so he finally had to get up and go to the fridge himself. It was the first time I'd ever caught him out of his chair. Anyway, he was so ticked that when he sat down again, he threw a stupid duck slipper at me!"

I could tell Past was trying not to laugh.

"It's not funny! The man is seriously annoying."

"The man needs counseling."

"The man needs a kick in the butt!"

"Okay," he said, still smirking, but covering it up by bending over his cart and pulling out camera equipment. "Let's get this place ready for Gladys."

I looked around the soup kitchen. It was a big white room with a linoleum floor like a school cafeteria, complete with tables and chairs. The walls were covered with peeling posters about churches and government agencies. It didn't look like the greatest backdrop for a music video. Fortunately, the kitchen, which was partially open to the rest of the room, had black curtains that could be shut to divide it from the eating area. We pulled them closed and set a chair and mike in front of them just as Gladys walked in.

She wrapped her arms around herself. "I'm not sure I'm good enough for YouTube."

"Come on, Gladys," I said, pulling her over to the

chair. "Have you seen some of the crap that's on YouTube? Belching, farting, people falling, lots less skill than you have. And I'm adding at the end what you're singing for, remember? We still need . . ." I tried to remember exactly how much we still needed for Misha's adoption. "Almost thirty-two thousand dollars. Hey! Has my dad deposited money in Moo's account yet?"

She shook her head.

"Are you kidding me?" I swung my arms out so violently, I almost knocked over the tripod and camera that Past had just set up.

"Mike!" Past yelled.

I grabbed the tripod, saving it.

"You can IM him later," Past said.

"Like it does any good," I muttered.

He paused. "Let's focus on Gladys."

Gladys looked positively horrified. She clutched the seat of the chair and I thought her eyes might roll back in her head at any moment. We tried saying, "Roll 'em!" several times, but she stared at the camera like a statue.

Eventually, Past went over and stood behind her, and I recorded him singing some old song called "Anticipation." Gladys didn't even react.

"That was a Carly Simon hit decades ago. This one is an R.E.M. classic called 'Losing My Religion.'" He really enunciated a line about singing, but Gladys still didn't move.

Finally, we heard a squeak.

"What?" I asked, running over to her so I might be able to hear.

"Stand," she whispered. "I think I need to stand?" It came out like a request.

I practically pulled her off the chair and stood her up while Past took the chair away. She wavered a moment, then stood still.

I ran behind the camera. "Okay, why don't you start by just saying hi, maybe introduce yourself."

"I'm Gladys." But that was all the talking she did.

All I could think was *She needs a better name.* Gladys was so . . . not like a cool singer. "I've got it! Your stage name is going to be Glad-Ice!"

A small smile crept across her face, ending in a laugh. "Glad-Ice," she said, nodding. "I like it."

Past turned the spotlights on her. Gladys's voice came out softly at first, but got stronger and stronger. By the time she'd completed her first song—a Billie Holiday number, she said—she was standing, relaxed and natural, and her voice was at a normal volume. And gorgeous. In fact, by the time I started recording, she looked completely cool. She moved—no, flowed—around the "stage" with the mike in her hand, belting out lyrics.

And, wow. The girl could sing. And not just sing. She was the complete package. An entire experience. An art form. She was the only person who could sing "The Itsy Bitsy Spider" and make it sound sexy.

And sultry. I discovered what *sultry* meant. Hot. Sweaty. The way I felt watching Gladys. When she moved on to "Love for Sale" and sang, "Who would like to sample my supply?" it was all I could do to keep from lunging at her. I had to suck it up, literally, when Past tapped my shoulder and said, "Mike, you're drooling on the equipment."

That kind of broke the mood. For Gladys, too. "Oh, no!" she said. "It's after nine! I was supposed to meet—be there by nine."

"Be where?" I asked.

She just shook her head and made for the door.

It wasn't the best ending to the night and I was a little bummed when Moo picked me up. Why did Gladys have to run off like that? Why couldn't she stay and hang out with us? With me. I kept thinking, *There's not that much of a difference between fourteen—going on fifteen—and eighteen.*

As Moo drove us home, she rattled on about her talk with Gladys earlier that day. "I told her those piercings are only to keep people away. And that her family may have been appalling but that going out with dope-heads isn't going to help her. I think I may have upset her."

"You didn't actually put it that . . . bluntly, did you?"

"Of course."

"Jeez, Moo! You can't come right out and say stuff like that! You have to approach it gradually and kind of hint at it."

"Mike. I don't have that much time left. I could be hit by a car tomorrow. You know the crazy way some people drive. Anyway, that Numnut is a convicted felon—Dr. P told me."

"The eye doctor? How would he know?"

"His brother-in-law is a police officer. Numnut was

convicted of"—she dropped her voice to a whisper—"car theft."

"Does Gladys know that?"

"I just told her today. I don't think she'll go out with him anymore."

"Well, she left the recording session to meet someone."

Moo's face turned as white as her hair. "And you didn't stop her?"

I sank down in my seat. I felt like I'd failed Gladys. "She said she had to get somewhere by nine and she was going to be late. I don't really know where—"

"Big Dawg's."

I was going to ask how she knew, but all I could do was hang on as I saw both yellow sneakers jam on the brake pedal, fishtailing Tyrone around to head us back the way we came.

19

OUTLIERS

—values far away from most of the others in a set of data

I convinced Moo to bring Past with us to Big Dawg's. I was underage and I wasn't sure they'd let her in that kind of a place, either. Unfortunately, Past insisted on loading the contents of his shopping cart into Tyrone, making me crazy.

"Would you hurry up?" I urged.

"Patience, Mike," Past said. "I need to—"

"MOVE YOUR KEISTER!" Moo yelled, and Past picked up the pace tenfold.

Tyrone squealed onto the road while Past crouched in the back with bottles, camera equipment, and, I guess, the entire contents of his cart. He braced himself against my seat back so hard, he was pushing me forward.

"Can't Tyrone go any faster?" I asked.

Seconds later, we skidded into Big Dawg's parking lot, almost hitting an entire row of cars before parking illegally behind several more.

Past was frozen in the backseat, so Moo and I ran for Big Dawg's door. I could hear the booming music coming from inside.

The bouncer had large tattoos on even larger arms, a sleeveless black tank top, black and gray camo pants, body piercings including earring links that formed a chain, a grim face, and squinty eyes. He stood in front of a black Camaro, his arms outstretched as if to protect it, probably from Tyrone.

Moo looked at him through her owl glasses. "Excuse me, dear, do you know Gladys?"

He squinted at me. "He can't come in. Too young."

"Oh, he's not coming in. He'll wait out here." She patted the guy's massive arm and he flinched. "You two can chat while I'm inside."

His eyes widened. "You—you don't want to go in there."

"Oh, but I have to," said Moo. "I'm looking for Gladys."

He gave me one of those is-she-for-real looks. "I think you're at the wrong place."

"No," said Moo, "I'm sure this is it."

"Uh, lady, what would a friend of yours be doing here?"

"Hooking up with Numnut."

The bouncer jerked back, almost hitting his head on the metal awning over the door.

"Gladys is eighteen," I said.

"Ohhh," he said, looking at Moo. "Well, what does she look like?"

"Oh, she's a lovely girl. She has beautiful eyes—"

"Spiked black hair with glitter," I interrupted, "a nose ring, tongue piercing . . ."

He looked at me and I realized he had all those things, too.

"Okay, she's about my height, great body, big lips, perky—" I cupped my hands in front of my chest.

"Mike!" Moo was staring at me.

The bouncer shrugged. "About half a dozen girls like that inside."

"And she's with this guy who's . . . really hairy, and has a band," I said.

Moo reached for the door.

He stepped in her way. "Are—are you sure you want to go in there? I mean, it's not like a beauty parlor, you know."

"I've watched Steven Seagal in *Under Siege* sixteen times," said Moo, trying to push past him. "I can handle this."

The bouncer stared at her.

"If you don't get out of my way," Moo warned him, "I'll call the cops!"

The bouncer flinched again, this time banging his head on the door. "Ow! Jeez, lady, I'm just trying to save you from—"

"From what? What's going on in there?" Her voice was rising and getting shrill. "I need to see Gladys! I need to see my Gladys!"

"Hold on," a calm voice behind us said. "I'm the one going in."

I turned around and saw Past, his arms crossed over his jacket, which looked a little bulkier than usual. "I'll go talk with her. You guys go on home. I'll get the rest of my things—" He coughed. "I'll get my things out of Tyrone later."

"Oh, no, dear," Moo said, "I want to talk with Gladys."

Past rubbed his forehead. "Moo, if you go in there, she's going to think you're checking up on her. How do you think that's going to make her feel?"

Moo chewed her lip. "But I—"

"I really think you need to let me handle this," Past urged. "It's not the first time she's gone back to Numnut, and she knows what everyone thinks of him. And of her."

"Yeah, why do girls do that, anyway?" the bouncer asked.

"Well," said Past, "it's usually because of insecurity and—"

"Hey!" I interrupted. "Could you postpone the analysis session, please?"

"Right," said Past, turning back to us. "I'll make sure she's fine, and I promise to let you know what happens."

Moo reluctantly agreed to leave, although she had to start Tyrone several times. "Oh, dear. We're low on gas."

I groaned, then remembered what Gladys had said about Dad *still* not depositing any money in Moo's account. I had Moo go back to Past's office so I could get Wi-Fi and convinced her she didn't need to be an antenna. So she busied herself taking Past's things out of Tyrone and putting them back in the shopping cart.

I had to shake my Pringles antenna several times to get a signal.

"I think the Pringles are all gone, Mike," Moo said, "but if you need a snack, I can get you something from Junior."

"It's a Wi-Fi antenna," I explained.

She stared at me for a moment before putting the cooler in Past's cart. "Of course it is, dear."

Before I IM'ed Dad to remind him about the money, I noticed the e-mail from Karen. She thanked me for all the wonderful work I was doing, specifically the almost ten thousand dollars we had so far. The LEGO bridge was all the way to Spain, nearing the Atlantic Ocean! She also said Past told her what a smart kid and problem solver I was. Ha! Who knew? Sure, it wasn't the kind of "problem solving" Dad valued, but her e-mail made me feel so up—she even said I was "brilliant"—that I couldn't help feeling kind of important. And I decided to tell Dad. Good thing he's always up at the crack of dawn, since it was barely 6:00 A.M. in Romania.

I even got a little excited as I IM'ed Dad all about Misha, like he might actually be proud of me. I had this fantasy that he'd say what I was doing was even more important than math problems, more important than a magnet school, more important than engineering itself.

It is not a wise idea.

Sometimes I can be such an idiot.

Even though it was admittedly bizarre that a kid would be put in charge of something as critical as adopting children, it still stung a little for him to say that. I knew I had to tell him that there were adults involved, that I was sharing the position with Past. Of course, I couldn't let on that Past was a homeless guy. That definitely would not be a wise idea.

Well, there's a guy, an adult, I'm working with, too.

Quite apart from a minor being in charge of such a project, the project itself is unwise.

Excuse me? Adopting kids is UNWISE?

There are too many unknown elements. A foreign country and system, for one.

I could feel myself getting more and more irritated with each line of his text.

You don't know anything about this child.

How dare he say that? I thought about the photos I had, and the eyes. "The Itsy Bitsy Spider" started running through my head. Just thinking about the video, I realized how much I knew about Misha. I knew this kid like I knew myself! I felt like shouting at the screen.

Yes, I do know him! I know all about him. I know he's kind to people, he doesn't like being ignored, he finds a way to take care of himself and his friends. I know he likes LEGOs and he built a LEGO bridge. I made you a LEGO bridge, Dad, but you probably don't remember that.

There was such a long pause, I thought he'd gone offline.

I remember. It was April 17th, the day before my birthday, at 3:40 in the afternoon. It had rained for two days, but that afternoon the sun came out.

I wasn't sure what to say. Or feel. Maybe he really did

remember. But the wrong details. Facts and figures. Not feelings.

How do you know all about this boy?

Misha, Dad. His name is Misha. Can you even say his name? It's not that hard.

How do you know about Misha?

Observation.

Observation?

From watching a DVD of him at the orphanage.

No response. I looked at my own words. *Watching a DVD?* That sounded so lame. But I *did* know him. I *saw* how he acted. I *felt* what he felt. I *knew* what he knew.

Nevertheless, you should focus your attention on Poppy's project.

Look, Dad. Misha is really doing something special for this town. He's breathing life into a dying place. People are getting excited. Karen needs him. People need him.

That is too much pressure to put on one boy who is unlikely to be able to live up to what's expected of him.

I felt my heart beating faster and my teeth gritting.

What are you saying, Dad?

You say that he is not a baby, but a school-aged child? Like you?

Younger than me, but yeah.

Then he is probably academically challenged.

What? Because he's like me?

He's already partly grown and has been in an orphanage.

Sasha came from an orphanage, remember? You think he's brilliant!

Ah, but he grew up with a family ever since he was a baby.

What about me?

I don't understand the question.

I took a deep breath and gritted my teeth.

So, if Misha is "academically challenged" we shouldn't care about him?

That is a moral question. I am speaking scientifically.

I discovered what that expression *to feel your blood boil* meant. Mine was about 212 degrees—Celsius!

Do you ever speak any other way than "scientifically"?

I'm not sure what you mean.

I know.

You should drop this project and work on something more beneficial. The artesian screw. That was the whole point of this trip. I would like an answer on—

I stopped reading. And gave him his answer.

Good-bye, Dad.

I shut down the IM window and stared at the wallpaper I'd put on the laptop—Misha's face.

20

CHAOS THEORY

—a branch of mathematics that deals with systems that appear to be orderly but in fact have chaotic behaviors

Moo was fretting about Gladys as we drove home in Tyrone, but I barely heard her. All I could think about was Misha. And Dad. And how he made me feel worthless. Even worse, now I felt like my goal was out of reach. I mean, I was academically challenged, a complete failure with numbers. It was a joke for me, a kid with dyscalculia, to be in charge of a project with so many numbers. Trying to raise *money*? By a certain *date*? For a kid some number of miles away but I still couldn't tell you *how many*?

I hung my head and touched my thumbs and forefingers together in my lap, making a circle. Like the sun. I remembered the orphanage video, with Misha's earnest face perfectly framed in his hands as he held them up and shouted, "Sun!" so proudly. I just couldn't let the kid down. It would kill me. Slowly, I held my hands up in front of me as "The Itsy Bitsy Spider" played in my head, and I tried to see Misha's face.

I stared through my joined hands, but what I saw through Tyrone's windshield wasn't Misha. It was another kid.

"Moo! Look out!" I grabbed the wheel just in time for Tyrone to miss a woman pushing a stroller with a little kid in it across the street.

Moo was hysterical, even worse than the mom, who explained that her son had colic, so she had to walk him at all hours of the night, but she "didn't expect to be *killed*." It took a while for me to get everyone calmed down enough for the mom and kid to go on their way and Moo to drive home at about fifteen miles per hour.

Moo must've said, "I didn't see them at all!" about fifty times before I finally got her up the front steps and into the living room. Poppy stared at her while I explained what happened, but he didn't say a thing.

I knew what had to be done, and I resented the fact that it was me doing it when it should have been Poppy. I took a deep breath and sat Moo down on the living room couch, hoping that Poppy might jump in and save me. Ha!

"Moo. You really need to go see Dr. P. You've got to get your eyes checked."

She bowed her head, nodding slightly, and pressed her lips together.

I glared at Poppy.

She sniffled, and when she spoke, her voice wavered.

"I'm scared of what he might say. I don't want to lose—" Her voice rose to a squeak. "Tyrone." She stood up quickly. "I need to vacuum now."

I glared at Poppy again. He blinked and looked at Felix.

As Moo vacuumed upstairs, Poppy flicked the TV on. A *Jeopardy!* rerun started. I couldn't believe that he could just sit there and watch TV while Moo was falling apart.

I so wanted to give Poppy a hard time, but I wasn't sure how.

Alex Trebek provided the answer. He was just starting to read the question from a particular category: Vegetables.

I sat down on the couch. "Hey, Poppy, look! It's your category."

I saw his eye twitch, so I kept at it.

"Yep, I'd go straight for the thousand-dollar question, because you're an expert in the vegetable department."

Another flicker.

"Do you want to try it out? Then say, 'I'll take Vegetables for a thousand, please, Alex.' And remember to phrase your answer in the form of a question."

I couldn't believe how mean I was being. And how easy it was.

When one of the players picked the vegetable category again, I acted all excited. "Listen to Alex, Poppy! Here's your chance to really score big."

Alex read the question. "This building, made entirely of corn, is constructed each year in South Dakota."

I jumped off the couch. "Corn Palace! I know this one! Sasha went there last year. Dude, say, 'What is the

Corn—' Oh, man! Too late! Judy already answered. Come on, dude, you're going to have to answer faster than that if you want to get anywhere in *Jeopardy!*"

Poppy's jaw clenched and his feet wiggled in his duck slippers.

I could still hear Moo blowing her nose over the noise of the vacuum and the TV. I glared at Poppy, who turned up the volume.

Alex read another vegetable question.

"Come on, Mr. Potato Head," I said to Poppy, "try this one."

He didn't answer, and his eyes narrowed even more when I called him "Broccoli Brains."

In Double Jeopardy, there was an ethnic foods category. "Hey," I said, "this could be your lucky day, because that scrapple, dude, that is one ethnic food, all right."

Alex read a question about some delicacy including sheep's eyeballs. "See, it's scrapple! Am I right or am I right?"

Poppy's hand clutched the arm of his chair and he snorted. He glared at me and I glared right back. It was a staring contest and I won it easily.

By the time I turned back to the TV, a contestant was saying, "What is 'Go jump in a lake,' Alex?"

"Correct!" Alex said. "And now you see the importance of phrasing your responses in the form of a question. Imagine how I'd feel if you just said, 'Go jump in a lake, Alex!'"

The contestants and audience started laughing. Meanwhile, I could hear Moo crying even over the sound of the vacuum. I stared at Poppy and got all mad again that he wouldn't do anything or even react to anything. So when Alex asked a literature question and the answer was Rip Van Winkle, the guy who fell asleep for twenty years, I yelled, "See! Just like you, YOU OLD STIFF!"

Only, Moo was in the living room by then and shut off the vacuum just in time to hear me yell, "YOU OLD STIFF!"

"Mike?"

"It's—uh—*Jeopardy!* I was just, you know, answering one of the questions."

She didn't say anything. But she looked over at Poppy and it was, well, a kind of tough look, like maybe she was getting sick of the way he was acting, too. She turned and headed for the kitchen, but I was hoping Poppy was withering inside like when the principal gives her Death Stare that, even if you shrug it off on the outside to look tough, still leaves you shaking on the inside.

When I walked up the steps to go to bed, I was sure Poppy was glaring at me. I felt the daggers in my back. Then I saw a duck slipper soaring through the air and felt it clip my shoulder. It hit the bottom step and let out a squawk. Yeah, I was finally getting to him.

21

ARGUMENT

—a variable that affects the result of a function

The next morning was the Fourth of July. There was no time for barbecues or fireworks because we had work to do. At Past's office, I uploaded the videos of Gladys singing while he filled me in on what had happened at Big Dawg's.

"I smuggled in the video camera. If I know one thing about abusive people, it's that they don't want their actions recorded for posterity. Or for the police. Gladys was embarrassed and left, and Numchuck pretty much clammed up because even he isn't stupid enough to show his true colors on camera. Of course, the bouncer kicked me out because of the camera . . ." He stopped and looked at me. "So, what's eating you this morning, Mike?"

To be honest, I was mad at Dad for what he'd said about Misha. But I figured Past would give me some kind of lecture I didn't want to hear, so I told him the other bad news, about the almost-accident and Moo having to get her eyes checked and maybe even having to give up Tyrone.

"It's time, though, Mike," he said. "It's not safe for her to be—"

"She's coming!" Guido hissed, running up to Past's bench.

Past jumped up, quickly checking the street. "Moo?"

"No," said Jerry, "the blond bombshell!"

Spud said nothing but had a grin from ear to ear, just like a porch pal's.

"Who?" I asked.

"Oh, right!" Past said. "The reporter! She wants to interview you because she's amazed you're so young."

Jerry was right. She was a blond bombshell in red spiky heels and a short, tight beige dress that made her look naked until you took a second look. And you wanted to take a second look. At least at the chest area, which was, shall we say, abundant.

I stood up, too, and all five of us stared.

"Hi," she said in a sexy voice. "I'm Whitney. An elderly woman told me I could find you here." She smiled at me.

"Moooo," I mumbled.

She stopped smiling. "Excuse me?"

"Moo—Moo—my great-aunt. That's what we call her."

The three stooges all murmured their Moos, which didn't help the situation. Whitney was looking less and less friendly.

Fortunately, Past saved the day. "We spoke on the phone, Whitney. Thank you so much for coming."

Whitney's face melted as he shook her hand and she was caught by his Bono eyes.

I leaned against Past's cart, which was beside his bench.

It was a mistake. Being a reporter, Whitney noticed. She looked at the shopping cart, then at us, suspicion in her eyes.

Past played it cool. "Ah, yes." He smiled and looked across the street. "The soup kitchen is over there. We feed a lot of homeless. This is a public park and . . ." He shrugged at the cart.

"I understand," she said. "They have to have someplace to go, don't they?"

He kept smiling smoothly, although he started blinking rapidly.

"So," I said, in an effort to get her suspicious eyes off of Past, "you wanted to ask me some questions?"

"Yes." She turned to me. "What got you interested in adoption, Mike?"

"Uh . . ." My mind had gone blank. "Well, he needs a family, right?"

"Misha?"

"Yeah."

"What's his story?"

"He has no parents, or they can't take care of him." I folded my arms. "Or won't. I don't really know the whole story."

"What's your story, Mike?"

I looked around at the others for help. "I—I don't know."

But Whitney was a reporter. That wasn't good enough for her. "I mean, what would drive a fourteen-year-old boy to work so hard on an adoption? There has to be some reason," she persisted.

I swallowed hard. "I just think a kid should have a family. That's all."

Her eyes were boring into me. "Why?"

My face was burning. I swallowed again and almost choked. My eyes darted around and I saw the photo of Misha on Past's cart. That was it! Divert attention. I pulled the photo of Misha with his LEGOs out of my pocket and showed it to her.

"Oh, that is so sweet," Whitney said in a baby voice.

I didn't like the way she made him sound like a puppy. "He's building a bridge," I said.

"A bridge?"

"Yes."

She examined the picture more closely. "Maybe it's a house. Yes, that's what it is, don't you think?"

"No. I think it's a bridge." I felt my teeth clench. Didn't she see the cars in the photo? What made her think she knew what was going on inside his head?

"Mike," Past whispered. "Why don't you tell her how much money we've raised and how much we still need? And the deadline?"

"Yeah," I said, except my mind was blank. I couldn't think of any numbers at all.

Fortunately, Past filled in the blanks for me and continued chatting with her about Do Over Day. All I could do was stand there stupidly and stare at the photo of Misha.

I finally snapped out of it when Whitney got in my face and asked, like maybe she'd asked the question once or twice already, "How did you get a homeless man to give up his shirt?"

I looked at Past, then quickly looked away. "Uh, he's really nice and he wanted to help."

"That is so touching." I swear there were tears in her eyes.

"It is," said Past, straight-faced.

"I wonder if I could do an interview with him."

I looked at Past. Past looked at the three stooges. The three stooges looked at each other.

"I think he's pretty busy," Guido offered.

"Yeah," I said. "A lot of these guys have jobs, you know. They just don't make enough money to have a place to live."

"Yeah," said Past, "and I happen to know he's working to get himself off the street."

Whitney looked disappointed, but she wasn't getting anything more out of us. After telling us the article would appear in Friday's paper, she assured us that the local TV station would want to cover Do Over Day.

The three stooges assured her that she needed a tour of Do Over, and possibly lunch, so they escorted her off.

When she was out of earshot, Past said, "Well, I think we'll get a story out of that." He cleared his throat. "I'm not sure exactly what kind of story, but we'll get something."

I realized then that I still didn't know Past's story. He seemed to know a lot about me. All I knew was that he was homeless. I turned and looked at him. "How did you become homeless, anyway, Past? What happened?"

He didn't answer.

"You're obviously smart. You're educated. What gives?"

He shook his head, his jaw set, and looked at his Clarks.

"I mean," I pressed him, "you just don't seem . . . homeless."

He took a deep breath, then said very quietly, "I'm not homeless."

I remembered Moo saying that, but then . . . "Okay," I said slowly, "so if you're not homeless, then why—"

"I just don't want to go home." He said it so softly, I could barely hear him.

What did that mean? He sounded like a kid who'd run away from home. "Why not?"

He took another deep breath and let it out slowly. His eyes were blinking so rapidly, he finally closed them altogether. "Because she's not there."

She? Who was she? His wife? His wife left him? What, he was divorced and couldn't handle it? People got divorced all the time. And handled it. They just divided up their stuff and dealt with it. "So, you're saying you have a house?"

He nodded, his eyes still closed.

Wait. I knew what happened if you didn't make your monthly mortgage payments on your house. The bank would take it back. And if he hadn't been working . . . "Are you losing your house because you haven't been paying the mortgage?"

He winced and shook his head slowly. Finally, he spoke. "Others have been making the payments for me."

"Others? Who others?" Who pays for somebody else's house? When he doesn't even live in it?

"Poppy and Moo, for one. Karen. The guys you call the three stooges. And—"

"Whoa, whoa! Back up a minute. Moo? Moo is paying your mortgage?"

He nodded.

"Moo, who's busting her butt and can barely scrape enough money together to feed herself—you're letting her pay your mortgage? And Karen? Who's trying to make money to adopt Misha? She's paying your mortgage while you're—you're out on the street . . . finding yourself or something? Dude! Are you out of your mind?"

He scraped the sidewalk with his Clarks and I wanted to stomp on them. "Believe me," Past said, his voice a hoarse whisper, "I feel terrible about it. I just couldn't handle things. I even had to send Joey away—"

"Joey?"

"He was the only family I had left, but—"

"I don't believe this! You left him? What a hypocrite!"

His eyes flashed at me. Hurt. Bewildered. Guilty.

"That's not building a family! First you're ruining Karen's chances of building a family, and then you walk out on your own family?"

"Joey's being well cared for."

"You didn't want to keep him yourself?"

"Of course I did! I do! I just—the street is no place for—"

"Then you shouldn't be on the street! Especially when you have your own home! Jeez!"

"Look, I can understand why you'd be upset."

"You understand nothing! You're making poor people pay for your house while you hang around supposedly working on building a family when you left your own! You don't get it at all!"

"Mike—"

"And telling Whitney some story about finding a job? That was all crap! *You're* all crap!"

"But—"

"I don't even want to talk to you. Leave me alone!"

He tried to touch my shoulder. "Mike—"

"Just—forget it!"

I took off, my Clarks feeling like clumsy lead weights and my LEGO brick chafing my thigh.

22

FUNCTION

—a special relationship
between values

I spent a long time walking and I didn't even know where I went or how I got home again. All I knew was that it had to be late because it was almost dark. When I went inside, there were no lights on. I jumped back when I saw the shadowy figure, a miniature version of Poppy, sitting on the couch. After I found the light switch and flicked it on, I saw who it was. Moo.

"Moo, what are you doing? It's pitch dark in here."

"It doesn't matter." Her voice was dead flat. "I'm blind, anyway."

"What?"

"Mac-you-lar jee-jen . . . jee-den—"

"Macular degeneration?" That was bad. Sasha's grandmother had that and wasn't allowed to drive.

Moo's voice was shaky. "That's it. I can't see. I can't drive anymore. I can't do anything." She sniffled. "I couldn't even drive Tyrone home. He was so upset."

"Tyrone?"

"No. Dr. Perr—Perr—Perrello. Two *r*'s. Two *l*'s." Her voice was squeaking steadily upward. "No *i*'s!" She covered her eyes and burst into tears.

Oh, jeez. I sat down on the couch and put my arm around her HOLY COMFORTER hoodie. She felt so frail as she shook with sobs. Moo without Tyrone? He was like a friend, especially since Poppy wasn't.

I felt like crap. Maybe if I'd just left things alone, she'd still have Tyrone, still have her life. She looked suddenly so old to me. Like a skinny elderly lady in an assisted-living place.

She gulp-cried and shakily put Tyrone's keys down on the coffee table.

"Where's Tyrone now?" I asked her, then immediately wanted to kick myself for asking. "At YE—Dr. P's, right?"

She nodded, crying so much she couldn't speak for a moment, and I sat there feeling my throat swelling.

"I don't know how to bring him home!" she wailed.

"Don't worry, Moo, we'll get Tyrone." Somehow. "Why don't you"—I ran to the closet and pulled out the Hoover—"vacuum."

She nodded, hobbled over to it, and dragged it into the kitchen.

I heard a choking sound from Poppy before the whir and dust balls of the vacuum started.

"What are you going to do about it?" I asked him, my eyes narrowed. "You could drive, you know, if you just got your butt out of the chair!" I grabbed the keys from the coffee table and stomped over to him, jangling them in his face.

He jerked and took a deep breath. For a moment, I thought it was working. He actually raised his right arm but then let it drop on the armrest again and sank even lower into his recliner.

"Come on! Go get Tyrone! Moo can't! It's one thing you could actually do for her!"

I felt my breathing, heavy and fast. I heard the keys jangle in my hand because I was shaking so much. I smelled his scrapple and sweat.

He scratched his head and turned away. "No," he grunted.

He finally spoke and that was all he could say? *No?*

I yelled the first thing that came into my head. "Why don't you go jump in a lake!"

I slammed the door after me, took the porch steps in one leap, and headed for Tyrone.

I pulled Misha's photo out of my pocket and put it on Tyrone's dash for good luck. With a deep breath, I put the keys in the ignition and turned on the engine. I'd warmed up our car for Dad before. How much harder could it be, really, to drive? Besides, it was dark and no one would see me. Who would even know?

Tyrone was parked in a spot where I could pull straight out, so leaving the parking lot was pretty easy. Staying on the road was a lot harder. From behind the steering wheel it looked like Tyrone took up the entire road. And

I mean *the entire road.* I don't know why they have that line down the middle because, basically, a car needs both lanes. Every time I tried to keep Tyrone to the right, he'd hit the gravel of the shoulder and lurch left again. And there must've been something wrong with his headlights because they kept moving around the road like he was trying to follow a tennis match in the dark.

Still, I thought I was doing pretty well until I saw the flashing lights and heard the siren. I let fly a string of colorful words.

I ground to a halt on the shoulder and put my window down, cringing as I watched the officer in the side mirror striding up to Tyrone, knowing that "objects in mirror are closer than they appear."

I smelled the garlic before he opened his mouth. "Evening, Moo— Hey! What the—! Who are you? And where's Moo?" He stuck his whole face in the window— dark, pointed eyebrows and large, sharp nose. And garlic.

"She's okay—she's at home."

"So you stole her car from under her nose?"

"I'm not stealing it! I'm taking it back to her."

"Oh, I get it. You're just borrowing it, huh? Well, kid, that's still stealing."

"No—"

"What's your name?"

"Mike Frost. I'm her—"

"Mike? Jeez. Her grandnephew? And she thought you were some kind of miracle. Who would've thought her little miracle would steal from her?"

"I'm not! She can't drive anymore because the eye

doctor said she has macular jee—gen—jee—" I was having as much trouble talking as Moo. "Mac-u-lar de-gen-er-a-tion."

"Uh-huh, okay. Did you stop and think to, oh, say, maybe have an adult drive the car?"

I was so mad at his attitude that I wasn't scared anymore and spat out my response. "Oh, sure! Like who? Poppy?"

"Is he still frozen?"

"Think iceberg."

He shook his head. "Even so, Mike, what made you think you could drive a car? I mean, you don't look old enough to have a license. Am I right?"

My shoulders drooped and I nodded.

He sighed. "Stay here." He took a step toward his patrol car, then his head was back in Tyrone's window. "On second thought, give me those keys."

I took them out of the ignition and handed them over. He walked back to his patrol car, muttering, "Maureen will never believe this one. Maybe she's right—I should write a book!"

I heard the radio crackling in the patrol car and sighed, staring at Misha's picture on the dash. What were his eyes telling me? I imagined what he might say. Like maybe I'd completely blown his chances. If I got arrested, who would take care of saving him?

When Tyrone's door opened, I jumped.

"Slide over, Mike."

"What?"

"You don't mind if I drive, do you?"

I scrambled over to the passenger seat. "Are you arresting me?"

"Why? Do you want to be arrested?"

"No. But—where are we going, then?"

He shook his head, grinning, as he started Tyrone. "Back to Moo's. Where do you think we're going? Disney World?"

I turned and looked out the back window. "What about your patrol car?"

"Well, the only car thief in town is here with me."

"I'm not a car thief!"

"Oh, yeah, I keep forgetting. You know, Moo has had a rough time lately. She doesn't need more heartache from you."

"Me?" I snorted. "I'm trying to help her! Which is a whole lot more than Poppy's doing."

"That's too bad he's not snapping out of it. I'm real sorry about that."

I looked over at him. He was frowning and shaking his head, so I figured he understood. As a cop, he must've seen all kinds of losers.

"What do you do with people like that?" I asked him.

"Me? I just shoot 'em."

"What!"

"I'm kidding."

"Dude, you shouldn't say stuff like that!"

"Uh-huh, and you've never done anything you shouldn't have? Like, oh . . ." He whipped his head to the right to glare at me. "Drive a car?"

I looked away. "What's going to happen to me?"

"Nothing. Unless . . ."

"Unless what?"

"Moo decides to press charges."

I let out my breath. "She won't. I was just wondering . . . what happens when someone drives without a license."

"Oh, that. Yeah. Thanks for reminding me."

Why didn't I just shut up?

"Depends. I think in your case we'll assign community service."

I knew it was a good deal, but I was wondering how I could do anything beyond Do Over Day.

He coughed. "I'm thinking you could work on, you know"—he pointed at Misha's picture on the dash—"getting ready for Do Over Day."

I felt my whole body sigh with relief.

He turned his head to look at me. "Sound okay?"

I nodded, trying to contain my smile.

We turned into Moo's driveway and I braced myself for the crash into Poppy's Suburban that never came.

"You're a little high-strung, aren't you, Mike?"

A patrol car pulled in right behind us, its siren piercing the night for just a moment, and I jumped.

He grinned. "Don't panic. That's just my ride." He tossed me the keys. "Inside. Now. No driving. Next time, I'll lock you up." He held his hand out to shake mine. "I'm Tony, by the way. You can call me Officer Giancola."

I shook his hand. "Yes, sir, Officer Giancola."

"And Mike?"

"Yes?"

"Good luck bringing that kid home."

23

ATTRIBUTES

—characteristics or qualities of an object

When I got inside, Moo was standing in the kitchen doorway, pulling on her hoodie strings.

"Mike?"

"I'm okay. So is Tyrone." I hung the keys on the peg near the door.

She nodded but kept yanking the strings. "Where's Poppy?"

"What?" I looked over at his chair. Empty. It was an unusual sight, and creepier than it was with Poppy in it. It even made the hairs on my arm stand on end.

"Mike?" Moo's voice was almost a wail.

"Maybe he's in the bathroom." Even as I said it, I knew it wasn't true.

Moo made a halfhearted effort to look up the stairs to the bathroom and shook her head. She knew it wasn't true, either.

"Maybe he went to bed early?"

She shook her head again, not even bothering to go and check. We both knew he wasn't there.

I swallowed hard. My heart was beating fast. I never thought I'd care if Poppy was gone, but I felt really cold and suddenly freaked, like when you're in one of those underground caverns and you've already got goose bumps from the cold and then they turn the lights out and you're not sure for a moment if they'll come back on again.

"Where is he, Mike?" Moo whispered. "Where would he go?"

Go? Where would Poppy go? Suddenly, I felt even colder. And my toes started wiggling in my Clarks. Did he go where I told him to go? *Why don't you go jump in a lake!* Like . . . Lake Revival? Oh, jeez!

"I'll be right back," I said, running past her and opening the kitchen door to the backyard.

"Where are you going?"

"To find Poppy."

"Mike?"

I turned to look at her.

"Thank you for being here. I don't know what we'd do without you."

I ran all the way down the hill in the dark, stumbling and tripping so many times I lost count. I didn't care; it was all forward progress whether I was running or rolling. I felt sick thinking about what Moo had just said. Was she thanking me for drowning her . . . I didn't even want to think of it. I had to find him.

When I reached the lake, I saw them. Duck slippers. Their little heads were facing the water as if yearning to go in, to follow the big duck that had gone off alone.

Oh, no. "Poppy! Poppy!" I yelled across the lake, then up the shore and down. "Poppy!"

No answer. I threw the Clarks off my feet. One of them hit a duck slipper, which gave a sick, plaintive squeak before it keeled over on its side. I swallowed hard, tore my gaze away from the duck, and waded into the lake.

I was up to my thighs when I realized my jeans felt incredibly heavy. I figured I'd swim in my boxers, but when I started to pull my jeans off, they were so wet they got stuck. It was an effort just to yank them up again. I kept waddling forward and finally dove into deeper water.

There's something weird about swimming in a lake in the dark. When you're underwater you're not quite sure which way is up. It's dark above you and below you and if you're swimming freestyle so fast you're overturning, and practically corkscrewing, you get disoriented and feel like you're floating in space. Even the feel of the air and the water start mixing and being the same because you hit pockets of cold and warm in both of them. You don't know what's up or what's down. You're pushing through space in a different kind of universe. And you don't know which way to turn.

I stopped, gasping, and treaded water. "Poppy!" I pushed the wet hair out of my eyes and blinked. I turned around in place, trying to let my feet do all the work to keep me afloat so I didn't make noise splashing. "Poppy!"

I heard a swooshing rush of water and spun around to face the noise. "Poppy?"

There was just enough dim moonlight to see what looked like a bent-over figure, maybe two figures, on the shore. Maybe one of them was Poppy. Or maybe it was an animal. Disoriented as I was, I figured out it was the other side of the lake from where I'd entered. I couldn't see the shape anymore and figured it had collapsed. I tried to fix my eyes on a particularly tall tree near the point I'd seen the form and swam at it as fast as I could, hoping that it was Poppy, hoping that it was still breathing, hoping that it would stay alive until I got there. I ran through CPR instructions in my head. *Repeated chest compressions. Press chest down two inches each time. Stay calm.*

When I got out on the other side, there was no lump on the shore. But I did see some dark marks in the moonlight, like huge wet footprints. I followed the marks, wobbling because my bare feet weren't used to walking over pebbles. I reached the line of trees and heard a particularly loud creaking sound above the random creaking of branches in the breeze. I looked up.

It would've been a funny sight, this old man sitting up in a tree with his legs dangling, a porch pal on the branch next to him, sitting as still as he was. Except it was scary. Because what was he doing up there? Getting ready to jump?

I didn't want to startle him if he was thinking of jumping. I spoke in a soft voice. "Hey, Poppy. What's up?" I cringed after I said it. I had to avoid words like *up* . . . and *down*.

Poppy put his arm around the porch pal. "Name's Doug."

Oh, man. He'd lost it. Now he thought he was Doug. Or did he think the porch pal was Doug? His dead son?

"Right," I said, positioning myself under the tree where I could see Poppy and the porch pal through the branches, the moon lighting them up like they were under a spotlight. Maybe if he saw a person below him, Poppy wouldn't jump. Or maybe I could break his fall. I moved closer in to the tree. "Hi . . . Doug."

Poppy lifted the porch pal's arm and waved it at me. The porch pal dripped on my head.

I ducked momentarily, then looked up again, in time to get a drip in my eye. I stepped away from the tree to get a better view and avoid the dripping porch pal. "Why don't you climb down?"

Poppy's face was pale and ghostly in the moonlight. He lifted the porch pal and sat it on his lap. When he spoke, his voice sounded different, kind of pouty and . . . like a kid. "My tree. I can do whatever I want."

I tried to make my voice sound casual. "Can I come up and join you?"

"Nope. My place. Nobody can bother me here. Not even my dad, dang pain."

"Yeah," I said, "I know what you mean."

I heard the branch creak as Poppy looked down at me.

He'd lost his devil horns. I guess the water had plastered his hair down flat. But I imagined his face was still grim.

"My dad is a pain, too," I said quickly. "Probably worse than yours."

"Nope. He's mean."

"Oh. Mine's . . . clueless."

He didn't say anything for a while, and I thought I'd better keep him talking. "And mine's always in my face, wanting me to be an engineer."

"You're lucky."

"How's that?"

"My dad was too busy for me. On the road all the time. Barely talked to me."

What could I say to that? It sounded like Poppy, all right.

"Yeah, well, it's no fun disappointing your dad all the time. It's better if he doesn't realize you're not what he wants." I swallowed hard and looked up at him. "Not that you're not what he wants, of course."

"Never even went to Kmart together."

I squirmed. I didn't know if it was Doug who felt bad that he didn't get to go or the dad, Poppy, who felt bad for not asking him. "Well, most kids don't really like shopping."

Poppy sighed. His voice cracked. "I miss him. I really miss him."

He gave Doug a squeeze and it was as if a small rain had started, splattering me with water from Lake Revival. Poppy's voice was barely a whisper as he said again, "I miss him."

I still wasn't exactly sure who Poppy was talking for—himself or Doug. Whoever it was wanted me to say something. I thought about what it would be like without Dad. I wondered if he'd noticed that I hadn't been IM'ing him. If so, he could've called. I'd given him the cell phone number. I kind of knew how Doug and Poppy felt, so I said what either one of them would want to hear. "Yeah, well, I bet he misses you, too."

"You think so?" He answered right away, like he'd been waiting for me to say something.

"I know so." At least, I hoped so.

Then it was quiet. For a long time. I kept an eye on them to make sure there was no movement, but all I heard around me were the other sounds of life: crickets, frogs, owls, the breeze picking up, leaves rustling, branches creaking. That last sound made me think that Poppy should get down from that tree soon.

I saw lightning in the distance and heard the low rumble of thunder. It actually smelled like rain. Heavy and wet. I could even smell the pine of the trees around me, along with the slight scent of vinegar from my wet U2 "Vertigo" T-shirt.

I looked at Poppy's tree more closely and saw remnants of pieces of wood, like ladder rungs, nailed to the trunk. So that was how an old guy could get up there. "Hey, Poppy? I mean, Doug? Is this the tree house you guys built?"

"Was."

"This is so cool! I saw a picture of it." I thought of the

photo of Poppy and Doug in happier times. "That's something you guys did together."

"About the only thing."

"That's a pretty big thing. If you did that, I can't believe you never did anything else."

He grunted. "Sometimes we played ball."

"See? You guys had some fun together."

"We never had fun. Never horsed around."

Jeez, there wasn't anything I could say to make him feel better. How long was this going to go on? The breeze picked up and I started shivering. I figured Poppy must be, too, and that it probably wasn't good for an old guy to be up there all wet. When the creaking of branches grew louder, I knew I had to make a move. I called up to him over the stiff breeze, "How about climbing down now?"

"Not ready."

I saw more lightning. "Sometimes you don't feel ready, but you have to move anyway."

"Don't have to. My tree. My life."

A flash of lightning followed by a clap of thunder sent a charge right through me and I suddenly felt my heart racing and my teeth gritting and my hands balling into fists. I didn't feel worried about Poppy anymore. Or sorry for him. I was angry. I wanted to shake him. I wanted him to get down from that tree so I could shake him into action. Enough with the self-pity already! He had to stop. Because what he did, or wouldn't do, wasn't just about himself. It affected other people.

"What about Moo, huh? What about Misha?" I yelled up at him.

Even my yelling didn't get his attention. He just shrugged.

That made me even madder.

"This isn't just about you, you know!" Then it hit me. "You're doing it all over again!"

This time he actually looked down at me, along with Doug. I didn't even mind Doug dripping on me.

"You're mad at yourself—or your dad—because of not living life and sitting around ignoring things, even when there were plenty of opportunities to do something. Well, guess what. That's exactly what's happening now!"

I gave him a little time for that to sink in as I paced in front of the tree and listened to the sound of thunder moving closer.

When I heard another sigh and more drips from Doug, I stopped, put my hands on my hips, and stared up at the two of them on the branch. My patience was gone. I could tell because my voice was sharp now. "It's time to move, Doug."

I heard Poppy let out a long breath. "Doug's gone, Mike."

"Yeah," I said, "I know. But Moo's still here. And Misha could be here if you'd do anything about it. It's time to move. Now!"

I heard all the air go out of him and the branches creak again before he turned around and slowly, stiffly stepped down the slats of wood one by one, with Doug over his shoulder. He didn't look at me once he reached the ground and we didn't talk, but somehow we both knew we didn't want to swim back the way we came. We walked all the way around Lake Revival, stopping to put on my Clarks and his duck slippers. As I tied up my shoes, I watched the breeze make ripples on the water that the moon turned into flickers of light. I remembered how dark the lake was when I'd sat there with Gladys. It looked bright now. I hoped it was a sign. I finished tying my shoes and felt my pocket for the LEGO brick, thankful that I'd taken Misha's photo out of my pocket and put it on Tyrone's dash. I shoved my hand in my pocket. It felt weird. I pushed my hand in deeper. Nothing. It wasn't there.

I started looking around the shore, crawling on the pebbles, looking for a hint of blue.

"Lose something?" Poppy asked.

"Yeah, it's a . . ." I stopped, realizing it would sound really stupid for a fourteen-year-old to be searching for his LEGO brick. I looked around quickly. The moonlight was bright enough to see a blue LEGO brick. Maybe. Then I remembered trying to take my jeans off in the water, then pulling them on again. Oh, no . . . the LEGO must've come out of my pocket. No, it wasn't possible. I stared out at Lake Revival, a big patch of darkness. My LEGO brick was gone.

"What'd you lose?" Poppy said, louder this time.

I stood up and shook my head. "Nothing." I stared at the lake. "Let's go."

I told myself it was just a LEGO brick and I could get another one from the box under my bed, one that had also been used to build that bridge, but it still felt weird. Like I'd lost something significant. I kept looking back at the lake, but pretty soon it was completely obscured by trees and I just had to move on.

We could see Moo silhouetted in the kitchen doorway for a while before she could see us. She kept running to the door, then running to the stove, then peering out the door again. She looked so frantic that I was about to call out to her when Poppy's hand gripped my shoulder.

"Mike, let's not say anything to Moo about the tree, okay?"

"Hey, it's your secret, right?"

"Our secret."

"Poppy!" It was Moo's shrill voice. "Is that you? And Mike? And . . . ?"

"Yeah," I called. "It's all three of us!"

She flung the door all the way open and came running toward us. "Thank goodness you're all right!" She hugged us, squeezing more water out of Doug. "What happened? You're all wet. Did you fall in the lake?"

I hadn't thought about how to explain that. I looked at Poppy. "We were just . . . horsing around."

"In the water? At night? With your clothes on?"

A streak of lightning lit up the sky.

"We'd better get inside," I said.

She looked so bewildered that I quickly changed the subject. "Hey, do you have any scrapple? We're starving!"

She beamed. "I made a whole panful!"

I brought Doug around to the front porch and sat him on his bench. I noticed the Life Is Good cap on the swirly rug next to the bench. It must've fallen off when Poppy took him on his little adventure. I thought about the three stooges' note—*He'll bring you good luck*—and stuck the cap back on his head. In a way, I guess Doug did bring us good luck. At least we'd gotten Poppy back alive. Even if it had cost me my LEGO brick.

From the front door, I saw Moo's yellow sneakers scurrying around the kitchen table, heaping scrapple on Poppy's plate, then on mine. I went in and sat down opposite Poppy, noticing that his hair was still flat but his eyes definitely had life in them. After Moo poured two glasses of powdered milk, she sat down between us, grinning from one of us to the other.

Poppy picked his fork up and my toes tingled just in time for me to get the message to pull his plate away. "Wait!"

Poppy stared at me, his fork in midair. "Huh?"

I pointed toward the pass-through. "First, put some new batteries in Felix."

Moo took in a sharp breath and lost her grin. She stared at Poppy, her eyes wide.

Poppy's fork still hung in front of him.

"Batteries are in the fridge," I said. "Top drawer. Behind the butter."

Moo was gripping her hoodie strings, frozen except for her eyes, which were burning. At Poppy.

He pushed himself away from the table, undid the bungee cord from the fridge handle, fished around inside, and came out with two AA batteries.

Moo and I stood and watched him through the pass-through as he slowly took Felix off the wall and worked at taking the old batteries out and putting in the new. When he put Felix back up on the wall, his hands were shaking, but so was Felix's tail.

Moo squealed and clapped, her yellow sneakers racing into the living room. I saw her stretch her arms wide, her hoodie blaring HOLY COMFORTER, as she pulled Poppy into a hug.

24

VARIABLE

—a quantity that can change or vary, taking on different values

Poppy went straight to the workshop to make his "dang boatload" of boxes to save Misha. Yes! There was still time for us to get some orders before the July 15 deadline! Moo and I stared after him. It was weird to see him with a mission. Heck, it was weird just seeing him move.

Moo was dancing, she was so happy. She hugged and kissed me about a dozen times. "Thank you, Mike! You brought Poppy back! I just can't thank you enough!"

"Moo, it's okay, really." I was still feeling guilty for being the one who sent Poppy to the lake in the first place. At least it had all worked out in the end.

"You are just a miracle! You're a URL!"

"What?"

"The Unwanteds Rescue League! You rescued Poppy! You're rescuing Misha! You're a wonderful friend to Gladys and to Past—especially to Past."

I sat down, put my head on the kitchen table, and groaned.

"What's wrong, dear?"

"You don't know what I said to Past."

"What did you say?"

I groaned again, and told her everything. "I wish I'd known he wasn't homeless."

"I did tell you, dear, but you didn't believe me." She sighed. "I'm afraid he took to the street after Natalie died."

"Natalie?"

"His wife."

"She died?"

"Yes."

I groaned again. "I thought they were just divorced."

"Oh, no, dear. She died at only thirty-three. It was such a shock. Past took it very hard. Natalie owned the health food store and jogged every day. No one could've been healthier."

I raised my head slowly. Natalie. All those flyers in his cart. Natalie's Natural Products. "That's why he's such a health nut!"

Moo nodded.

"But," I realized, "she died anyway, so why does he still try to be healthy?"

"She died of a heart condition that no one even knew about. If she hadn't led such a healthy lifestyle, she probably would've died much earlier."

Images of Past ran through my head—typing at his

office, talking with Whitney, doing the "Three Bears" video, standing with his cart in front of Natalie's Natural Products . . . "All that stuff in his cart—is that from her health store?"

Moo nodded again. "He lost her. He lost the store. He lost his life, really. He was in training to be a lay minister. Natalie encouraged him. People were already calling him Pastor . . . until Natalie died and he told everyone to shorten it to Past because his life was in the past."

I thought about how I'd yelled at Past because I'd just assumed his wife walked out on him and he couldn't handle it. I cringed. Natalie had died. Why didn't I think of that? Me, of all people. I knew about death. And the aftermath. "What about Joey?"

"He's staying with Natalie's parents until Past is ready to handle him again."

I hung my head and sighed. "I feel really sorry for the poor little guy."

"Oh, he's not so little. And he smells."

"Moo!"

"And drools, and he sheds something awful."

"Wait a minute. Is Joey . . . a dog?"

"Of course, Mike, what did you think he was?"

"A son."

"Oh, dear, no! Well, I can see why you'd be so upset with Past, then."

I put my head in my hands.

Moo tried smoothing out the hair on top of my head.

Why was she so nice to me? To everyone? I looked at her. "Moo, why were you paying his mortgage when you guys can barely get by as it is?"

"I was always friendly with Past and Natalie, but after Doug died"—she stopped and took a deep breath—"and then Natalie died, well, I really felt for Past. Besides, I have my URL to keep up, remember?"

"Oh, yeah." I thought about Moo taking care of all the unwanteds. "Is that how you ended up with me for the summer?"

"Oh, my dear, I begged your father to send you to visit for years, but he'd never do it. He didn't want to part with you."

"Uh, Moo, Dad sent me here because he didn't want to be stuck with me in Romania."

"That's not true, Mike."

"Yeah, actually, it is."

"No, he said he'd already lost his wife and he couldn't do without his only child for a whole summer."

"What? He said that?" Was she sure? It sounded like some other father.

"Yes. That's when I asked him, 'Can't you go teach abroad somewhere? Isn't that what professors do?'"

"You asked him?"

"Yes. Of course, I knew the answer already. Professors do go teach abroad. I learned that on *Oprah*."

"But . . . why did you want me here?" She'd never even met me.

"Because your father is . . . different. And life with him must be a little . . . unusual." A smile spread across her face until her full set of dentures showed and her eyes sparkled behind her vinegar-clean glasses. "I wanted you to see what life was like in a normal family." She paused, still grinning. "Do you like being in a normal family?"

I looked through the pass-through at the working Felix, ticking twenty minutes after eleven. Now that I'd brought Tyrone the car back home and gotten Poppy the vegetable out of his chair and into his workshop, I needed to go find a homeless guy who wasn't really homeless and see if I could get him to move back into his house, which was being paid for by a little old lady who could barely afford scrapple. Normal? I shook my head and stood up to go find Past.

Moo's grin faded and she tugged her hoodie strings. "Oh, dear. We're not too boring, are we? That's it, isn't it? We're too dull!"

"No! Not at all. *Dull* and *boring* are about the last words I'd use."

Moo beamed. "I'm so glad, dear!" She squeezed my hand and peered into my eyes. "One more thing. I want you to have Tyrone."

"What?" I sat down again with a thump and stared at her. I couldn't imagine Moo without Tyrone. "I couldn't do that. You love Tyrone."

"And you do, too. I know, because you risked getting arrested just to bring him home."

"I—I'm not really supposed to be driving yet."

"I know, so he'll live here until you're old enough. But"—she grinned so much, her shoulders went up to her ears—"I know you'll come and visit him. In fact, you can bring your dad with you at Christmas, maybe Thanksgiving, too, and definitely over the summer."

Dad? If Dad came here, he'd find out about the artesian screw. Or lack thereof.

"Won't that be fun? You'll get to meet Misha, too! And see Past."

Past. "I need to go talk to him." I just hoped this rescue would be as successful as Poppy's.

25

UNFAVORABLE OUTCOMES

—the odds that an event will not succeed

I ran all the way to Kmart before I had to slow down to a walk. The rumble of thunder grew louder. The heat lightning that lit up the clouds earlier was turning into real lightning in the distance. And real rain, soft at first but rapidly getting heavier. My T-shirt, which had almost dried since Lake Revival, was soaked again.

By the time I could see the park, it was pouring, the rain splashing mud in tiny fountains where the grass didn't grow. The park looked surreal in the dark, like a completely different place. The full moon lit up Past's office like a spotlight and the flashes of lightning made it almost disappear into ghostly whiteness for brief moments. As I got close, I saw that his cart was gone and his bench was empty except for a large beige envelope. When

I reached his office, panting, I picked up the envelope. It had my name on it, or what was left of my name since the rain had made the letters run into an eerie version of *Mike*. I grabbed the envelope and ripped it open. Inside I found Past's cell phone and a note.

> I need to go. I think I've taken care of everything I can. I know you'll take care of the rest. You'll do fine without me, Mike/Misha.
>
> —Past

I looked for any kind of message or sign on the phone. There was none. I stuffed it in my pocket that used to hold my LEGO and stared at the note. I don't know how many times I read it, but with each reading I felt less guilty, less sorry, less sad. And more angry. Sure, I felt terrible for him, about his wife. But, I mean, look at Moo. Her son died and she was still taking care of herself— and Poppy, and Gladys, not to mention Past's house. Even when she lost her best friend, Tyrone. Past was young. He was healthy. He ought to be able to handle things without running away.

I stared at the note again. *I need to go?* Yeah, like when the going gets tough, the tough get going . . . out of town. *I think I've taken care of everything I can.* What did that even mean? Was there some paperwork he didn't do? More than likely, considering his next sentence: *I know you'll take care of the rest.* The rest of what? The paperwork? The money? Do Over Day—including the food and the chorus that *he* was supposed to be handling? *You'll be fine without me*—I swallowed hard—*Mike/Misha.*

How would I be fine on my own? How would Misha be fine? He wouldn't! Not unless we got the money and met the deadline. And if not . . .

I kicked Past's bench. What an idiot! He was just going to abandon Misha? I kicked it again. What a complete idiot! I jumped up on the bench, nearly slipping, it was so wet, and stomped up and down on it, splashing the standing water, yelling, "IDIOTS!" as loud as I could, like I was the wacko homeless person, but I didn't care. I was mad at all of them—Past for abandoning Misha, Poppy for taking so long—too long—to start helping, and even Moo. Why did she keep making excuses for Poppy?

"IDIOTS! All of you! Don't you know what really matters? Not running away! Not hiding from things! Not covering things up! But doing what you know is right! For Misha!"

I jumped off the bench and squelched into the mud, sliding several feet before falling on my back next to some bushes. My head landed next to some papers—the math worksheets from Dad that we'd been using to print up flyers for Do Over Day. Seeing the math worksheets just made me angrier. I got up and kicked them, stomped all over them, ground them into the mud. I had so much adrenaline, I wanted to destroy every piece. I stomped so wildly that some of them flipped over. And Misha stared up at me.

I froze. Oh, no! I didn't know these had already been

printed with Misha's picture! I bent down to pick up a muddied, torn flyer. The boy in my Buzz Lightyear T-shirt stared back at me. Those eyes. The look that said, *Mike, don't you get it yet? Don't you see?*

"See what?" I said to the picture, my voice high-pitched and crackling, my breathing rapid because of all my jumping up and down. Misha just kept staring at me, but no matter how long I stared back at him, I still had no answer.

26

TRANSFORMATION

—moving a shape to a new location

I couldn't sleep that night. I paced around the tiny bedroom until I felt sick. Looking at the photo of Doug and Poppy in their tree house didn't help. Thinking about what I'd done for Misha didn't help. I kept remembering his torn picture and hoping it wasn't a sign.

I saw the lights were still on in the workshop, and I needed company. Any company.

Poppy looked up when I opened the door. "One big dang mess in here," he muttered.

I slumped against the door. "At least I cleaned up the nails. There were a lot of them."

He shrugged. "Ever heard the expression 'so angry you're spitting nails'?"

"Yeah . . . but it doesn't mean actually spitting nails."

"I don't spit. I throw."

He wasn't kidding. About two minutes later the jigsaw blade got tangled and he grabbed a handful of nails, throwing them against the far wall of the shop.

I flinched.

He grunted. "I heard about Past."

I didn't say anything. How much had Moo told him? Everything about what a jerk I'd been?

"You like yelling at people, don't you?"

She'd told him everything. I sighed and sat down on a sawhorse.

"Don't sit on that!"

I jumped up. Why had I come in here, anyway? I glanced over to see what he was doing. "What are you working on?"

He looked at me like I was an idiot. "What do you think?"

"Boxes?"

He grunted. "A genius. Like your dad." The jigsaw blade got stuck again and Poppy's hand dove for the box of nails.

I dove for cover.

Poppy cleared his throat. "So your dad wants you to be an engineer."

"Yeah."

"You'd make a lousy engineer."

I stared at him. Did he have to be so blunt? "Because I suck at woodworking?"

Poppy squished his lips together and shook his head.

"Because I suck at math."

Poppy grunted. "Because you don't want to be one."

There. He'd said it. Amazing. He understood more than Dad.

He glued the edges of two squares of wood together. "He'll be fine."

"Dad?"

Poppy snorted. "Couldn't tell you about him. I meant Past."

"How do you know?"

"I got experience. You gave him a kick in the teeth."

I cringed. "I know."

"Exactly what he needed."

I hoped he was right. I watched Poppy put a piece of wood through the table saw like he was slicing butter. He made it look so easy. I wondered if it would work if I tried. Nah. There were some things I just wasn't any good at. Like artesian screws.

Poppy looked over at me. "You still here? You should get some sleep."

"I'm not tired."

"That's what Moo said and then she crashed. Oh, her phone rang after she went to bed. It was that girl at the bank with all the screws in her head. She wants to know—"

"Wait a minute. You actually answered the phone." I couldn't picture that.

He grunted. "Can't stand that ring tone and I didn't know any other way to stop it. Anyway, she heard about the macular degeneration. She wants to do something for Moo." He paused. "Any ideas?"

I thought for a while about Gladys and Moo. And how important it was to Gladys for Misha to have a family because hers had been so crappy. "Yeah, I have an idea. You guys should adopt Gladys."

He dropped his sander on the floor. "We're too old! She's too old!"

"Not adopt for real, just kind of take care of her. Like, maybe when I leave, she could move into Doug's room."

Poppy was staring at me. I looked up at the sign Moo had posted above the workshop door: What Would Oprah Say?

Poppy followed my gaze.

"So, what do you say?" I asked him.

He grunted. "Maybe you should send her to Oprah. She'd fix her up good."

I folded my arms, stood firm in my Clarks, and stared at him. "You could ignore Gladys. And let another chance slip by. Until it's too late. Again."

I saw the air go out of him as his whole body deflated. Leaning his forearms on the workbench, he hung his head and spoke softly. "I wouldn't even know what to say to her."

"You start with 'Hi.' Maybe followed by 'Thanks for being a friend to Moo.' And then, 'You want to stay for dinner? Moo's cooking, so it's no skin off my nose.'"

He grunted. "Guess it wouldn't kill me."

I rolled my eyes. "That's really big of you, Poppy."

"Don't I know it." He went back to sanding.

"Hey, are you going to be able to get all the boxes done?"

He grunted.

"Is anyone else working on them? I thought you were leading a whole artisan's crew."

"They're doing the finishing work."

"There's over a hundred ordered. How fast can you get them done?"

He put down his sander again. "A dang lot faster if people would get out of my shop and let me work."

I grinned and started to close the door behind me.

"Mike?"

I put my head back in the workshop. "What?"

"Thanks," he muttered. He was concentrating hard on the box when he said it, but his hands weren't moving.

For a moment, I didn't know what he was talking about, but then I realized he meant talking him down from that tree. Or maybe sending him to that tree in the first place.

"Sure," I said. "No problem." My problem was Past. And Dad. And making sure Misha got here.

27

DEFECTIVE
NUMBERS

—numbers whose factors
add up to less than
the number itself

The next morning—ten days to Karen's deadline and three days to Do Over Day—I walked all the way to the park, borrowed the laptop from the soup kitchen, and sat down in Past's office. I updated the deadline and posted lots of blurbs about Misha and Do Over Day on Twitter and everywhere else I could find.

Thinking about Past's note and how much he might not have done, I tried calling Karen all morning, but she never answered. I left voice mails but I backed up my messages with a text, too:

Do you have all the paperwork submitted to the adoption agency? Are we meeting the

deadline? Let me know ASAP if there's anything I need to do.

I was practicing my deep grown-up voice, so I could call the adoption agency myself and check on the paperwork, when I got a text from Karen.

Sorry, Mike, I'm not allowed to turn the phone on in the hospital. I'm outside checking messages at the moment. Don't worry, though, Past is taking care of all the paperwork.

I'm not so sure about that. Past left town.

I know. He needs to take care of himself, and family matters.

Yeah, but what about Misha? Don't you need some Apostilles in Harrisburg? Do you want me to get Guido or one of the guys to do it?

But that's what he's doing.

Guido?

No, Past.

Past? But he's gone. And you just said it was to take care of himself and family matters.

His family AND mine. He drove all night to Ohio to pick up my paperwork, then drove to Harrisburg, then he's driving to New York to the adoption agency and to get some forms I need at the Romanian embassy. Isn't he a sweetheart?

I sat there, stunned. Why didn't he tell me? Past was not only taking care of his own family, he was also making sure Misha was going to get adopted. To say I felt like crap for thinking the worst of him would be an understatement. I don't know how long I sat there before I heard the three stooges. When I looked up, they were all staring at me. And they didn't look happy.

"Where's Past?" Guido asked.

"He had to go out of town to take care of stuff."

"When will he be back?"

"I don't know."

"Well, is he going to be back in time for Do Over Day?" Guido persisted.

"I don't know."

"What?" said Jerry.

"I don't know! Okay?"

"Testy, aren't we?" Jerry looked at Guido. "Someone didn't get his beauty rest."

"I have to go to the bank," I said, walking off fast with the laptop. I could've called Gladys to find out what was in our fund, but I didn't feel like hanging around with them.

At the bank, Gladys reported a total of just over fifteen thousand dollars.

"Well, there's some good news, at least," I muttered.

Gladys eyed me. "Any idea when Past will be back?"

"Why is everyone asking me?" I snapped.

She put her arms around herself and started rocking. I watched the guitar tattoo teeter back and forth. "What'll we do if he's not back for Do Over Day? It's only three days away. Do you realize how much we need him?"

Of course I did. I needed Past to direct the chorus. And take care of the food. And help handle the press. But mostly I needed him because, well, he was a friend. Even though I hadn't treated him like one.

"I bet he'll be back," she said, nodding as if she was trying to convince herself.

I sighed. As bad as I felt, the show had to go on. "If not, can you lead the chorus?"

"Me? I—I can play the keyboard. That'll help keep them on key." Her voice wavered. "No one would listen to me, anyway." She added hurriedly, "Not that I care. It's sort of like an understanding I have with . . . people in this town."

I looked at Gladys and remembered what Moo said about all her piercings and tough outer shell. "You can't hide forever, you know."

Her mouth dropped open and she stared at me like she was pretending to be angry when we both knew I was right. Besides, her blushing face revealed it. "I am not hiding!"

"Yeah, right."

"Oh, you're one to talk."

"What's that supposed to mean?"

"You're the one who's hiding."

"Me? I'm not hiding from anything!"

"Except your father."

"I—I—" I didn't know what to say.

"It's so obvious. You don't want him to know that you're not a genius."

"He knows I'm not a genius. He can tell that from my grades. Trust me."

"Maybe, but he still thinks that's what you want to be. He thinks you want to be like him. As long as he believes that, then there's no risk, is there?"

"Risk? Risk of what?"

"Risk of losing him, too. Of having no family."

It was like she'd punched me in the gut. I had no air inside me, yet I couldn't take a breath.

Her face softened and her eyes were sad. "Moo told me. . . . I'm sorry about your mom. And I'm sorry about your dad, for that matter." She cleared her throat and drew herself up again. "But don't accuse me of hiding when you won't admit—"

I slapped my hand down on my laptop. "You don't know what you're talking about!"

She shrugged and looked away, her shield back in place. "So why don't you tell him?"

"Tell him what?"

"That you don't want to be an engineer."

"Fine! I will! It's no big deal!"

She pointed at the laptop in my hands.

"What?"

She rolled her eyes and made a big production of turning her Mac to face me.

Suddenly, I felt cold. Like I was under a spotlight. I stood up. "I'll do it from my own office!"

I stormed out of the bank and headed for Past's bench. The adrenaline from my fight with Gladys was making my legs shaky. I felt hot and cold and sweaty, all at the same time. Who did she think she was, lecturing me like that? I wasn't scared of telling Dad I didn't want to be an engineer. That was crazy! I could do it whenever I wanted. It's just that, why would I bring up something that was going to annoy him? What's the point of that? He'd figure it out on his own, anyway. Or if he didn't, I'd tell him. Eventually. Really. It was no big deal.

I opened the laptop and entered the money that we'd made so far. And stared at Misha's face.

The three stooges were quiet, but I could feel their eyes burning into me. I opened up an instant message. And stopped. What would I say? I was getting no brainstorm from my toes. Should I tell Dad there was no artesian screw? Should I tell him it didn't matter? Because there was no way I was going to be an engineer? I didn't even want to be? What would he say? I finally decided to just start and see where it went from there.

Hey Dad.
Greetings! Finally, Professor son speak! No need for worry. Heart was bad but then he have operation. Is all over now.
What?! Who is this? Is this some kind of sick joke?
Joke is not sick. Father is sick. In hospital. Is OK now.
Who are you?!
Ferdi Petrescu. I am graduated student of Professor Frost. You are son, yes?
I am son. What happened to my dad?
My dad is OK.
Not your dad, MY dad!

I am sorry. My English not fluent. You speak German?

No.

Polish?

No.

I am guessing your Romanian not so good also. I am right?

Yes. Your English is good. Sorry. I'm just upset about my dad. How is he?

He is OK but fat. Doctor say must lose minimum 35 kilos.

How much is that?

Much. Is how much maybe 10 year old boy is.

You mean like 60 pounds?

No. Like 80 pounds.

Jeez.

I am sorry? I do not know what is "jeez."

Nothing. I'm just mad because I've been telling him for years that he should lose weight.

You are doctor?

No. I'm 14.

You are only boy. Professor do not listen to boy. Even boy student who is 23. I bring Professor fruit. Fruit goes to spoil.

He won't eat fruit or vegetables.

I think he change now.

Maybe.

This is big thing. He is lucky to live. He turn over new leafs now. He love his son, he say to me, so he promise to eat fruit.

He said that?

Yes, all kinds of fruit.

No, did he really say he loves his son?

Yes.

Are you sure?

Yes. Why you not believe?

**It's just not the kind of thing he says. Or
I say, either.**

Why? My father say he love me. I say to my father. Why is
wrong?

**It's not wrong, it's just that guys
I don't know
It's just kind of weird.**

I think is weird to not say. Jeez.

What happens now?

He say he love you, now you say you love him.

**No, I mean, when does he get out of the
hospital and that kind of stuff?**

I think maybe Friday. He want to talk to you. He is very
proud of son. You are mini engineer, yes?

Not really.

He say you want to be engineer like him.

**Yeah, that's what he says. Can I talk to
him?**

About engineer?

No, I mean, can he get on IM?

No laptop or cell phone in hospital.

But we can IM on Friday?

Yes. Now I must go. Good-bye.

Wait!

Yes?

Tell him hi for me.

I say you love, OK?

Yeah, OK. Thanks.

It was kind of hard to focus on Do Over Day after that. But I had a job to do. And there wasn't anything I could do about Dad. Yet.

28

INTERVAL

—the distance between two points

By the next day, Poppy had three different styles of boxes made, and I have to give the man credit. They were the most beautiful pieces of art I'd seen in a long time. I took pictures of them and went to Past's office to load them on eBay. I noticed Past's latest shirt had been bid up to $340! It's amazing what people will pay for stuff on eBay. Good thing, too, since that shirt might be the last one. Who knew when Past was coming back.

I posted the photos on the website, too, and updated our deadline—nine days!—and only two days until Do Over Day. I added another brick to the LEGO bridge. We were finally in the Atlantic Ocean on our way to the Azores, islands about one third of the way across the Atlantic from Europe.

I stared at the map of Romania. I thought about Dad in the hospital and Misha in the orphanage, and I hoped they'd both be out of those institutions soon. I decided to

IM Ferdi. I had to adjust the Pringles can several times before getting a strong enough signal.

He said Dad was doing okay many times, because I asked him about five different ways, just to be sure he understood. Then, I don't know why, I decided to tell him about Misha.

> You are in charge of project? You are genius like your father. I am moved to crying for the little boy who will have a mama now. It is great thing.

> **Yeah, it'll be great as long as I don't screw up big-time.**

> I think you do not screw up big-time. You are very smart boy, not big screw up.

If he only knew. If Dad only knew. But it was better that he didn't. I gave Ferdi the YouTube sites so he could take a look at what we were doing. I sort of wanted him to pass on the info to Dad. And I sort of didn't.

"Hey, Me-Mike!" Guido yelled.

I looked across the street to the soup kitchen, where the three stooges were dragging piles of flattened boxes into the building.

"What are you guys doing?"

"Packing porch pals," said Jerry. "We just got fifty-nine orders through eBay! You can add seventeen hundred dollars to the website!"

That was almost two LEGO bricks! I quickly updated the money goal and stretched the LEGO bridge closer to the Azores, then ran across the street to help. Inside the soup kitchen, porch pals were leaning up against the wall like a bunch of kids in a lunch line. Guido was assembling boxes while Spud packed them and Jerry filled out mailing labels. I took a spot beside Guido and went to work assembling boxes.

When we'd almost finished, I noticed a separate heap of porch pals. "What's with the pile in the corner?" I asked Guido.

He kept taping a box as he looked around. "Those are the rejects."

"What's wrong with them? They look okay to me."

"They're practice ones." He stopped unrolling a strip of tape long enough to rip it off the roll with his teeth. "If you look closer, you'll see poor stitching, stuffing coming out—just not good enough to sell."

I stared at the face of one of them. It had bushy eyebrows like Past. I couldn't help thinking about him and how much he liked these guys. They'd still make Past smile, even if they weren't perfect. That's when I got my idea. "Hey, can I borrow some of the rejects?"

Guido narrowed his eyes at me. "What for? We can't have any imperfects floating around the Internet."

"They're not leaving town, I promise. I'm using them for . . . advertising purposes."

He grunted. "I guess that's okay."

I gathered up the five imperfect porch pals and headed to the park.

Knowing that Past was handling the final paperwork for the adoption, I was feeling a lot better about that deadline. Now it was just a question of the money. And preparing for Do Over Day—I sure hoped kids liked bananas as much as Past seemed to think, and they wouldn't mind the all-natural version of M&M's, not to mention sparkling raspberry water. I got Guido to handle face-painting, Spud was supposedly a whiz at balloon animals, and Jerry would do magic tricks. The moms were happy to run the sack race, three-legged race, and egg-on-a-spoon race. Dr. and Mrs. P said they'd handle sales—everything from Moo's vinegars and Mrs. P's fruit spreads to Gladys's bling and the three stooges' porch pals. Dr. P even wanted me to make up a bunch of Pringles Wi-Fi antenna kits to sell because he liked the idea so much. It was hard to smile when he grinned and said, "I'll buy all the supplies and I'll let you eat all the Pringles!" I knew I wouldn't be able to eat the Pringles without choking, thinking of Past.

With all the craziness of organizing Do Over Day, it was the next afternoon before I got to Past's office to IM Ferdi again and check on Dad.

Dad is good. He wants chocolate. I say no. But nurse give him chocolate. Jeez!

Should he be eating chocolate?

If is good dark Romanian chocolate, yes. Otherwise, is trash. I send some home with your dad so you try.

Thanks.

Is least I do for someone who help orphan children. I watch YouTubes. Very good. This Moo is very funny. I like. My grandmother love. She buy 3 per week vinegar plan. Is good vinegar?

The best.

She also buy vinegar for gift for my father for birthday
next month. I have better idea for birthday. I think he will
very much like a wood box by Poopy.

Poppy.

Yes, Poppy. I order one today. Money goes to orphan family, yes?

Yes, all of it.

My father will like. Did I say, I see Misha video? He is good
boy, smart boy. He take good care of his friends. Like
you, I think, yes?

I try.

Good. I see your dad tomorrow. What I should say to him
for you?

**Tell him I hope he's feeling better. And
eating the right food.**

And?

What?

What is other good thing for son to say to father?

OK, OK. I love you.

I love you too, Mike.

Dude! I was talking about my dad!

I know! I kid you! I am funny, like Moo, yes?

Very funny.

I tell your father what you say. You IM maybe tomorrow
with him. I think he out from hospital then.

I tried to stop worrying about Dad. Instead, I worried
about Past. Moo and Poppy seemed smugly confident that
he was fine. In fact, their smirks at the mention of Past's

name made me wonder if they had inside knowledge. As irritating as it was to be out of the loop, I felt better thinking that Past was okay. And Poppy had gotten a new battery in his Suburban, so he was actually driving Moo around, which I felt a whole lot better about. For both of them. Things were looking up.

Until the next day.

29

TESSELLATIONS

—patterns of shapes that fit together without any gaps

Do Over Day dawned gray and threatening, and there was still no sign of Past. Even Moo didn't look quite as smug. I helped Poppy load his boxes and Moo's vinegars into the Suburban. When we were done, it started sprinkling. Raindrops made a plink-plunk sound as they fell in the plastic buckets scattered around the front yard.

We waited for Moo on the front porch, watching the rain get heavier and heavier. Poppy sat with his arm around Doug while I leaned on the handrail. Poppy pointed at Doug's head, now missing the Life Is Good hat. "Mike, do you know what happened to the hat?"

"Uh . . . yeah. I had to borrow it." I added quickly, "I don't think Doug will mind."

Poppy grunted. "It's a stuffed doll, Mike. Of course it won't mind."

Moo opened the front door and stepped onto the porch

with a proud grin. She was wearing a pale green sheet, her yellow sneakers, and a wreath headdress, looking like a Halloween costume version of Julius Caesar. Junior was slung over her shoulder.

I looked at Poppy, who only shrugged.

"Moo, why are you dressed like that?"

"It's my chorus costume. Some of us decided to wear international outfits to add some flavor."

"But . . . Misha is Romanian, not Roman, remember?"

"I know that, dear."

"Then why are you wearing a toga?"

She grinned and held a neon green flashlight high above her head. "I'm the Statue of Liberty! Can't you tell?"

We had to move Do Over Day into the soup kitchen because the rain wasn't letting up. Everyone was running around like crazy, and I mean crazy. The three stooges were dressed as wacky as Moo. It took me a moment to figure out that Spud was dressed as a porch pal dressed as the Pope. Jerry's skinny, hairy legs stuck out from under his leather shorts and suspenders. "My German grandfather's lederhosen from when he was a teenager—and I can still fit into them!" he announced to everyone who'd listen and those who tried to avoid him. Guido was dressed all in green, looking like a leprechaun, and sporting a large button on his chest that said, KISS ME, I'M IRISH!

"Guido?" I said. "Guido is Irish?"

"I'm Irish-Italian, a regular melting pot right here," he said, thumping his chest.

I had too much work to do to worry about the costumes. We got everything set up inside and I made sure everyone had what they needed at the various booths and that the food was in place. I'd already set up Karen's laptop and the one from the soup kitchen with a photo collage of Misha pictures and the video from the orphanage in an endless loop. With the projectors Dr. P got, I was able to use the opposite walls of the room as screens to show larger-than-life videos and photos of Misha.

On the other full wall that wasn't broken up with the opening to the kitchen, I put up my huge map of Romania to Pennsylvania. It was on butcher paper, compliments of the soup kitchen, and I did a pretty good outline of the countries of Europe and eastern North America. The moms had brought buckets of crayons and markers for kids to be able to draw the countries in different colors and the ocean in blue. I made the LEGO bridge myself, though, and we were now almost to the Azores, heading for Do Over, PA. Heck, we were so close to the Azores, we could probably swim there. On top of the last LEGO piece, I put a blown-up photo of Misha. I stepped back and smiled.

"It's lovely!"

I whirled around and there was Whitney.

"H-hi," I said, suave as usual.

"Tell me about your map. I see you used LEGOs, just like Misha."

I told her all about it. It was a lot easier to talk about something I really understood as Whitney scribbled away, and this time I even knew the numbers.

It wasn't as easy when I saw the TV camera. And

lights. And those huge boom microphones that look like horizontal black lampposts. And guys holding them, looking around for someone's mouth to put the mike in front of. So they picked mine.

Desperately, I looked around for Past. He'd know what to say. He was smooth. He even looked good. I glanced down at my Radiohead T-shirt with their song on it: "These Are My Twisted Words." Yeah, that was about right. I looked around for Past again. Still no luck.

The bright lights blinked in my face. I had to squint and shade my eyes.

A guy in a suit with lots of makeup on his face was smiling at the camera, saying my name and a bunch of other stuff that I didn't catch. Soon his smiling mug was next to mine and the mike was in my face.

"Uh . . ."

The guy's smile lessened just a little. "Maybe you can tell us how much you've raised."

"Oh! Yes, we have $19,853.88, but we need to raise forty thousand by July fifteenth." I warmed up fast, stopped shading my eyes, and looked right into the camera. "That's only one week from today, folks! We need your help!" I grabbed a flyer with Misha's picture from the table next to me and held it up in front of the camera. "He needs your help. This is Misha, the kid we're saving, and if you'd like to see a video of him, it's right over there!" I pointed to the wall that was showing the orphanage video. "He's a great kid. I know you'd love him if you just had a chance to meet him. Come on, send in your money to Bring Misha Home, P.O. Box 29, Do Over, PA, 159—"

"Do Over?" the news guy finally interrupted, laughing. "Don't you mean Donover?"

"It's Do Over for Misha." I looked at the camera again. "Come on, guys, this kid needs a home. Is that asking too much? Just a second chance, someone to believe in him."

"Perfect!" someone yelled. "That's a wrap!"

"Thank you, Mike!" the news guy said. "Good luck getting twenty thousand dollars in one week!" He turned to his crew. "Now, let's get the healthy snack angle." They all headed to the food table.

My heart sank at what he'd said. *Good luck getting twenty thousand dollars in one week!* Even I could do the math—that was almost three thousand a day. It had taken us two weeks to raise that much. It felt pretty hopeless. Not that I was giving up, but for the first time I felt, really felt, like this might never happen. Sure, I'd been scared about it before, but Past had been there, and there had been time, or at least it felt like it. Now . . . twenty thousand in one week?

I walked over to the map of Romania and Pennsylvania and looked at the photo of Misha sitting on his LEGO brick. In the middle of the ocean. I had to finish that bridge. Somehow. Do Over Day would make some money, and hopefully this press coverage would help, but . . .

A boy a little older than Misha, with unnatural pink stuff on his face that was definitely not Past-sanctioned food, stood next to me. I smiled at him.

He looked up at me and pointed to the map. "That kid is hosed."

My smile dropped and I stared at him. "What?" It came out as a whisper.

"The bridge ends in the middle of the ocean. He's history."

I found my voice. "No, he isn't."

"Yes, he is."

Something hot was bubbling inside me. I spoke through gritted teeth. "It's—just—a—picture."

"He's going to fall in."

I leaned down to the kid's level. "No. He's. NOT."

"Yes, he is. He's going to drown."

"HE IS NOT GOING TO DROWN!" I yelled, and the kid started screaming and wouldn't stop.

I tried to resist an insistent tugging on my arm until the loud voice in my ear prevented me. "MIKE, DEAR, WHY DON'T YOU COME HELP WITH THE CHORUS?"

I let Moo drag me across the room to where Gladys was trying to conduct the chorus, but I threw dagger looks back at the obnoxious kid, whose mom was shooting me an equally knife-like stare. I wasn't sure if the horrible noise in my head was because of that stupid kid or the chorus, but eventually I figured out that it was definitely the chorus. The singers were way off pitch because Gladys was trying to direct them, so she couldn't play the keyboard. I sent Gladys back to the keyboard and tried to start the signature song from the top.

Although the tonal quality improved noticeably, they

still sounded terrible, like they were all singing different songs.

I finally yelled at them. "Guys! I can't understand a word you're saying!"

Guido yelled back, "That's because they're *foreign* words, Me-Mike."

"It's not because they're foreign!" I said. "It's because you're all singing things at different times."

"We're supposed to. Each group has a greeting to say and we all take turns."

"But you're not taking turns! That's the point! It's all ONE BIG MESS!"

"What's wrong with him?" Jerry asked. "Get up on the wrong side of the bed?"

Moo was looking at me, chewing her lip. She tugged at her drapes where her hoodie strings normally were. "Mike, dear, it's all right. I'll lead the chorus."

Moo tried to conduct with her flashlight but she kept dropping it, hitting people's toes, until the front row was a line of defensive motion, which led to pushing and shoving and squabbling just like in elementary school.

"I say *shalom*!" Jerry insisted.

"No," said Guido. "You're supposed to say *ciao*. I'm in the *shalom* group!"

Jerry pulled on his suspender straps. "You're not a *shalom* anymore, remember? You switched with Moo because she can't pronounce *ko-nee—, ko-nee-wa—*"

"It's *konnichiwa*," said Guido, "and you obviously can't pronounce it, either."

"I know! That's why I'm a *shalom*!"

I closed my eyes, hiding from the bright lights of the cameramen, ready to give up. Was it possible to do over a Do Over Day? I didn't even need my MP3 player to hear a ringing in my ears and imagine the Proclaimers singing.

I was in such a state I was hallucinating, hearing Past's voice singing, the way he did when we were trying to record Gladys and she wouldn't sing. Now I was hearing Past's voice in my head singing "I'm on My Way" by the Proclaimers.

I shook my head and opened my eyes again. I tried to focus on the chorus so I could come back to reality, but they were staring at me. Or, actually, behind me.

I whipped around and there was Past, wearing the pink Life Is Good hat and singing about being on his way to happiness. The chorus erupted into applause, drowning out any chance I had to speak.

"Excuse me, Lady Liberty," Past called out to Moo, approaching the front of the chorus. "I'll take your tired, your poor, your huddled masses, and you can go on back to your spot, okay?"

Moo grinned and gave Past as much of a hug as her drapery would allow.

Gladys played her keyboard with great feeling and volume. I scrambled to get behind the camera and turn it on so I could film the chorus and post it on YouTube. Past waved his left hand to tone Gladys down as he used his right to point to the *ciao*s and the *shalom*s and every other group so that soon everyone was singing on cue, sounding like a polished bunch of professionals. Or, at least, really enthusiastic amateurs.

I watched Past conduct the Do Over Chorus, his pink cap bobbing up and down as he really got into it. And I looked at the collage of Misha photos on the wall behind the chorus, and saw the pictures of Misha, the kid who was NOT going to drown, while I listened to the chorus sing their song for Misha, "Hello to All the Children of the World."

We all clapped and cheered at the end. Moo waved her neon green torch as people ducked, until Past stopped her with, "That'll do, Lady Liberty!"

"Past," Moo called out, "what does the rest of that poem on the Statue of Liberty say? There's a line about lifting my lamp." She lifted her flashlight and people in the front row scattered again. "But there's another line, too."

I watched Past press his lips together and look up toward the bill of his cap in thought. A grin spread across his face. He searched for me with his Bono eyes and, finding my face, held it with a smile. "Send these, the homeless, tempest-tost to me."

30

ENDPOINT

—point marking the end of a line segment

Funny thing," Past said to me amid the bright lights, cameras, and commotion. "There was a porch pal at my office"—he touched the bill of the Life Is Good cap—"wearing this hat, as a matter of fact."

"Yeah?" I was happy to see that Doug's hat had brought good luck.

He nodded. "Another one pointing down the street. Then I saw one on the corner, pointing to another porch pal in front of my house."

I tried to keep from grinning.

"And what do you know? There was one sitting on the front porch. My front porch. What could I do? I had to go up and say hello. We had a nice talk."

"You talked to it?"

"Not it, Mike. Her."

"Sorry."

"It felt good."

I nodded. "I knew you liked those porch pals."

"I mean . . . it felt good to be back home. Thank you."

I shrugged. "I'm really sorry about yelling at you. I didn't realize—"

"I needed a little kick start. It was time." He looked down at his Clarks. After a moment, he looked up at me and a smile grew. "I have something to show you. Follow me."

Past led me to the corner of the room near the door where a large brown mixed-breed dog was sprawled. He thumped his tail and raised his head as soon as he saw Past. His mouth opened into what I swear looked like a smile.

"This is Joey."

As soon as Past said his name, Joey made a Wookiee noise like Chewbacca in *Star Wars*.

Past rubbed Joey's tummy as Joey rolled over on his back, closed his eyes, and let his tongue drop out the side of his mouth. Moo was right. He did drool. And smell. But he sure looked happy.

"He's in doggy heaven," I said, while Past was saying, "He's back with me now."

We grinned at each other.

"Same thing," I said. "Are you . . . back now?" I didn't know how else to say it. I didn't mean just back in town. I meant back in life.

"I'm back in the game. The Past is now the future." He touched the bill of his Life Is Good cap with his free hand and gave a little bow. "And I'm happy to report that Natalie's parents want to order a bunch of Poppy's boxes for Christmas gifts for, well, I think everyone they know. Over fifty boxes."

"Fifty! Fifty times two hundred is . . ."

"Ten thousand dollars."

"Ten thousand dollars? Ten thousand dollars! That means we hopefully only need to make ten thousand in the next week! Wait—are you sure they're buying that many?"

"They're going to try. Misha's adoption was important to Natalie, too . . ." His voice trailed off and he blinked hard.

"So," I said, "now she's helping to bring Misha home."

He nodded. "I felt awful about her store going out of business, but this is more of a legacy."

The Statue of Liberty burst in between us. "Did you hear? Oprah might contact me! Isn't that exciting?" She gave me a knowing look. "I bet you know how that happened."

"You sent her some vinegar?"

"No, silly! The TV reporter asked me if I'd like to say anything to the viewers, and I said, 'Oprah, dear, I really think you should get involved in this,' and that lovely newsman said he'd be sure to send a copy of the program to Oprah. Can you imagine? Oh, Mike! It would be a dream come true!" Lady Liberty was off and running. "Gladys! Gladys, I have to tell you about Oprah!"

Past surveyed the room and put a hand on my shoulder. "I've got to hand it to you, Mike. You really know how to engineer things." He smiled. "You brought Poppy out of his shell, you took a group of people who knew nothing about the Internet and got them on YouTube, you put a bunch of schemes in place to make money to adopt an orphan, I even heard that Gladys might be moving in with Poppy and Moo. . . ."

His voice went on, but I was hardly listening. Something he said made my toes wiggle inside my Clarks as I watched the celebration around me. Moo and Gladys hugging. The three stooges talking into a microphone in front of a camera. Poppy scowling at a reporter who was handling one of his boxes. Things really were coming together. We had almost half the money and more on the way. The publicity would help that. It was going to work. It had to work. We were bringing Misha home.

I stopped and stared at Past. "Wait a minute! What did you say?"

"I've said a lot of things, Mike. Which wonderful words of wisdom did you want to hear again?"

And then it hit me. *Engineer.* That's what he said. I had *engineered* things. I had made things happen.

I stomped my foot. That day on the beach when I was four or five—I still remember it—all the kids were fighting, no one could agree what to do, and I got them to work on building a sand castle together. No more fighting. Bringing people together. Making things happen. I was a problem solver. Not a math-problem solver. I engineered . . . life. That's what Mom meant! *That* kind of great engineer!

"Earth to Mike. Come in, please, sometime before the next century."

It was Past. All I could do was grin.

"Looks like you've had some great revelation. Either that or you're dreaming of porch pals."

I looked at the flurry of activity around me. The smiling faces. The energy. "This really worked, didn't it?"

He nodded slowly, smiling. "It sure did. Thanks to you."

Past definitely looked different somehow. Not exactly happy, but . . . less haunted, maybe? I noticed that he was wearing another new shirt. And a tie, even. And his jacket was a lightweight suit jacket, not a heavy tweed. "Where've you been, anyway?"

"Natalie's parents."

He told me all about visiting them and trying to help them come to terms with the loss of their daughter instead of being so self-absorbed and ignoring everyone else's pain.

I was still feeling a little guilty for yelling at him about not getting over his dead wife, even though I hadn't known she was dead. "Why didn't you tell me what had happened to you?"

Past avoided my eyes. "If I had, would you have had anything to do with me? Some self-centered guy who let other people suffer while he dealt—or didn't deal—with things? Or would you have written me off as another Poppy?" He turned to look at me. "Another Dad?"

It was my turn to look away.

"Not that I would've blamed you. I was behaving badly. But there's always hope, Mike. I'm changing. Poppy's changing."

"Yeah. I'm not so sure about my dad, though."

Past shrugged. "You and your dad are on different planes. He'll never be exactly who you want him to be."

I nodded. I wasn't exactly who he wanted me to be, either. Past had pretty much nailed it. The tough part would be telling Dad that. Somehow. Someday. Later.

I was telling Past about Dad's being in the hospital when Moo came running up to us again, in full grin mode, her shoulders touching her ears. "Isn't it exciting?"

I smiled. "Yeah. It sure is."

"Have you seen him yet?"

I looked at Past.

He looked away, blinking and covering a grin with his hand.

"Who?" I asked.

"Your father!"

31

ABSOLUTE VALUE

—how far a number is from zero
—absolute value is always positive

y dad?"

"Oh, there he is!" Moo's green drape dragged against my chest as she raised her arm. "Yoo-hoo! James! Over here!"

I turned and saw him. He was wearing a lightweight gray suit that I didn't recognize. He looked thinner. It made him look shorter, too, smaller all over. And his hair was grayer than I remembered. His skin was gray, too. He wasn't moving too quickly, either. It finally occurred to me that he was recovering from major surgery and an overseas flight, so he probably wasn't feeling so great.

I grabbed a chair from the table near me and pulled it toward him. "Dad! Dude, sit down."

He put his hand on the back of the chair and kind of wobbled into the seat. "Hello . . . Mike."

I forgave him for pausing before my name, because he'd

stopped to take a breath, which kind of sank out of him again as he sat. He was hunched over, looking up at me.

"Hi, Dad. I—I didn't even know you were out of the hospital."

"I asked Ferdi not to tell you. I wanted it to be a surprise." His voice was kind of raspy and soft. "And I wanted to get here for the big day, the unveiling of the artesian screw."

I looked at Moo, whose grin faded as she gathered up her sheets. "Let me find Poppy."

Past cleared his throat. "Uh . . . Professor Frost, I guess Moo didn't tell you—"

"It's okay, Past," I said. "I'll handle this." How, I didn't know. All I knew was that it had to be me.

Past bowed his head and backed away, accompanied by Joey.

Dad looked up at me. "What did Moo neglect to tell me?"

I took a deep breath and let it out slowly. "Actually, it wasn't just Moo, it was me. There—there isn't any artesian screw."

"Ah." He nodded. "Sometimes these designs don't work out in the end, but you can still learn a lot in the process. Did you find—"

"There never was an artesian screw. It was a misunderstanding. See, Moo sometimes says things wrong, and what she really meant to say was 'artisan's crew,' which was basically just Poppy building wooden boxes."

Dad stared at me for a moment, blinking, then turned away. "Boxes?" he whispered.

"Yeah. They're really nice boxes."

Dad's head turned back to me and I felt his disapproving gaze as I spiraled downward into the dumb-little-kid role that I'd always had with him. I couldn't let that happen. Not after this summer. Not after everything I'd been through. I had to break out of the mold.

"Nevertheless, working on boxes will hardly prepare you for—"

"I know, Dad."

"It's a good thing I came home when I did. We can go home and—"

"No! I'm not going anywhere. I'm in charge of bringing Misha home."

"Misha?"

"The kid who's being adopted!"

"Ah, yes. Ferdi told me more about that. It's quite amazing what you've done."

I tapped my Clarks nervously on the linoleum. *But useless.* I knew that was what he was about to add.

"I would never have attempted that," he said, shaking his head.

"Yeah, well, he's worth it, Dad! You might think he's *academically challenged*, but maybe he's good at something you're not. Or me. Or Poppy. Maybe he actually has value!" I grabbed a flyer and held Misha's picture up for him to see. "Look at him, Dad! Look at his eyes!"

Dad looked at the photo, at me, back at Misha, then back to me again. Did even Dad see it, too? The similarities between us?

He sighed. "It makes me think about your mother."

"Mom? Mom would've liked what I've done."

He nodded slowly. "Indeed, she would have."

I stared at him, wondering what was coming next. It felt like the whole room was quiet, where before it had been such a commotion. It seemed like everyone was watching me. And a boom mike was dangerously close to my head. I was sweating from the heat of the lights, the heat of the room, or something.

I turned back to Dad. He looked . . . disappointed. I couldn't stand that look. I raised my head, and above Dad I saw the video playing of Misha. And there it was. The part of the video where the woman with the milk pitcher goes offscreen and Misha looks straight at the camera. Straight at me. Staring. And right then, finally, I figured out what his eyes had been telling me all along.

Misha was taking a risk. A huge risk. He was plunging into a new life, leaving everything he knew behind. What if people didn't like him? What if it didn't work out? He couldn't go back. Nor could I. Once the cat was out of the bag that I didn't want Dad's life, I couldn't go back and pretend that nothing had happened. Somehow, I'd have to make it work on my own.

But then I realized something else. The risk wasn't that Dad would be disappointed. It wasn't even that he'd disown me and I'd be left with no family, no one. The real risk was even greater than that—if I didn't stand up and do what I wanted with my life, it would be like my life was just . . . lost. Over. Before it even began.

I heard Dad speaking, but I only caught the end of what he said. ". . . we'll stay another week so you can meet your fund-raising deadline. Then we'll go home and find an engineering project for you to work on. I'll talk with my colleagues in the engineering depart—"

"No, Dad!"

He flinched.

"The thing is, I'm not good at that stuff." I took a deep breath. "And really, I'm not interested. I'm not interested in engineering, or math, or anything like that. And I never will be." I looked at him. He just seemed stunned. "Sorry to disappoint you."

"But I can help you with those subjects—"

I threw my hands in the air. "I don't want your help! Don't you get it? I'm not smart that way, and I don't *want* to be."

Dad's face crumpled into despair or disdain, I didn't know which. Either way, it only made me angrier.

I hit my chest. "I'm Mike!" I yelled. "MIKE! And I'm not your kind of engineer. I'm the kind of engineer that makes things happen. A—a *life* engineer. Not numbers. Life! That's who I am!" I finally stopped to take a breath.

The room felt silent when I stopped. Even the reporters seemed to be holding their breath. While I'd felt like everyone had been staring at me, now they seemed to be staring at Dad.

He took his glasses out of his jacket pocket, opened them, and put them on. "I saw a boy—he was visiting at the hospital—who looked just like you."

What was he talking about? "Dad, you can't even picture my face, so how could he remind you of me?"

"Because he was with a woman whose walk reminded me of your mother's. He was approximately three years, ten-point-five months."

"Approximately three years, ten-point-five months? How did you come up with that?"

"Ah. I have a picture of you in my wallet." He reached inside his jacket, wincing slightly, pulled out his wallet, opened it up, and retrieved a photo. "On the back, I wrote the date it was taken. You were three years, ten-point-five months old."

He showed it to me. It felt kind of good that he kept a photo of me along with his credit cards and everything else, even if it was really old. "I could get you a more recent photo, Dad—if you want."

"No need."

My head drooped.

He put the photo back in his wallet and pulled out another. "I have every year of your school pictures in my wallet. Ten, including kindergarten and preschool."

"You have ten photos of me in your wallet?"

"No. I have seventeen. Some are from when you were very young, and three are soccer photos."

"Wow." Cool. So cool my throat hurt and my eyes were stinging.

"I know I have an imagery problem, so it's my way of compensating. We all have to learn those techniques."

I started to jump in, but he kept talking.

"Mike. Son. The reason I wanted so much to teach you math and engineering skills is simply that I can." He glanced around the room. "But look at what you've orchestrated here. And you're only *fourteen*." He emphasized *fourteen*, maybe to impress upon me that he actually knew my correct age. Or maybe because he really was impressed.

I was so stunned, I just stood there.

"You've inherited your mother's ability with . . . people. That's something I don't have. Math is something you can learn, but social skills, understanding people, knowing what to say—those are all things that are beyond me." He looked up at me. Maybe because he was hunched over, maybe because he was still recovering from surgery, or maybe because I felt different myself, Dad looked like a little kid. "Math, engineering, that's all I know."

For the first time in my life I actually felt, well, sorry for him. I didn't feel inferior. I felt like I had something at least as valuable as he did. Maybe I even had more. "Dad, I can teach you that stuff."

His forehead wrinkled. "Really?"

I nodded. "Sure."

I held my hand out to him, to shake his hand. He didn't extend his. Instead, he pushed against the seat of the chair, struggled to his feet, and awkwardly spread his arms into a hug.

I heard a sniffle behind me, followed by a Wookiee noise. I turned to see Past wiping his eyes and Joey kissing his hand. Past looked up, gave me a long Bono look, and nodded. I smiled back.

Behind Past, I saw Moo, her yellow sneakers peeking out from under her toga. And Poppy, clutching one of his boxes. And Gladys, sandwiched between them. And behind them, the video of Misha, holding his hands up in front of him and shouting, "Sun!"

Turn the page to sample Kathryn Erskine's
NATIONAL BOOK AWARD WINNER,

mockingbird

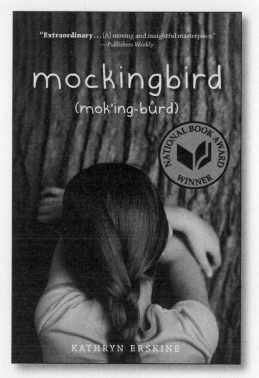

CHAPTER 1

DEVON'S CHEST

IT LOOKS LIKE A ONE-WINGED bird crouching in the corner of our living room. Hurt. Trying to fly every time the heat pump turns on with a click and a groan and blows cold air onto the sheet and lifts it up and it flutters for just a moment and then falls down again. Still. Dead.

Dad covered it with the gray sheet so I can't see it, but I know it's there. And I can still draw it. I take my charcoal pencil and copy what I

1

see. A grayish square-ish thing that's almost as tall as me. With only one wing.

Underneath the sheet is Devon's Eagle Scout project. It's the chest Dad and Devon are making so he'll be ready to teach other Boy Scouts how to build a chest. I feel all around the sheet just to be sure his chest is underneath. It's cold and hard and stiff on the outside and cavernous on the inside. My Dictionary says CAVernous means filled with cavities or hollow areas. That's what's on the inside of Devon's chest. Hollow areas. On the outside is the part that looks like the bird's broken wing because the sheet hangs off of it loosely. Under the sheet is a piece of wood that's going to be the door once Dad and Devon finish the chest. Except now I don't know how they can. Now that Devon is gone. The bird will be trying to fly but never getting anywhere. Just floating and falling. Floating and falling.

The gray of outside is inside. Inside the living room. Inside the chest. Inside me. It's so gray that turning on a lamp is too sharp and it hurts. So the lamps are off. But it's still too bright. It should be black inside and that's what I want so I put my head under the sofa cushion where the green plaid fabric smells like Dad's sweat and Devon's socks and my popcorn and the cushion feels soft and heavy on my head and I push deeper so my shoulders and chest can get under it too and there's a weight on me that holds me down and keeps me from floating and falling and floating and falling like the bird.

CHAPTER **2**

LOOK AT THE PERSON

CAITLIN, DAD SAYS. THE WHOLE town is upset by what happened. They want to help.

How?

They want to be with you. Talk to you. Take you places.

I don't want to be with them or talk to them or go places with them.

4

He sighs. *They want to help you deal with life, Caitlin . . . without Devon.*

I don't know what this means but the people come to our house. I wish I could hide in Devon's room but I'm not allowed in there now. Not since The Day Our Life Fell Apart and Dad slammed Devon's door shut and put his head against it and cried and said, *No no no no no.* So I can't go to my hidey-hole in Devon's room anymore and I miss it.

I try to hide in my room and draw but Dad comes and gets me.

There are so many voices in our house. Voices from Devon's Boy Scout troop. I recognize their green pants. And the nice things they say about Devon.

Voices of relatives. Dad introduces me to them. He says, *You remember . . .* and then he says a name.

I say, *No,* because I don't remember.

Dad says to Look At The Person so I look quickly at a nose or a mouth or an ear but I still don't remember.

One voice says, *I'm your second cousin.*

Another says, *Wasn't it a beautiful memorial service?*

Another says, *I love your drawings. You're a very talented artist. Will you draw something for me?*

One even says, *Aren't you lucky to have so many relatives?*
I don't feel lucky but they keep coming.

Relatives we hardly saw when Devon was here so how can they help?

Neighbors like the man who yelled at Devon to get off his lawn. How can he help?

People from school. Mrs. Brook my counselor. Miss Harper the principal. All my teachers since kindergarten except my real fifth-grade teacher because she left after what happened at Devon's school. I don't Get It because nothing bad happened at James Madison Elementary School so why did she have to leave? Now Mrs. Johnson is my teacher. She didn't even know Devon except she watched him play basketball, she says. Twice. I've watched the LA Lakers play more than twice. I don't try to help them.

Caitlin. If you ever want to talk about what happened you just let me know, Mrs. Johnson says.

That's what Mrs. Brook is for, I tell her.

Maybe we could all sit down together.

Why?

So we know where you're coming from.

I look around the living room and stare at the sheet-covered chest. *I come from here.*

I'm sorry. I meant so we all know how you're feeling.

Oh. Mrs. Brook knows how I'm feeling so you can find out from her. I would be superfluous. My Dictionary says suPER-fluous means exceeding what is sufficient or necessary.

I just thought it would be nice to take some time to sit and chat.

I shake my head. *SuPERfluous also means marked by wastefulness.*

Well . . . okay then, she says. *I suppose I can talk with Mrs. Brook.*

Mrs. Brook says you can talk with her anytime because her door is always open, I tell Mrs. Johnson. *Actually it's almost always closed. But if you knock then she remembers to open it.*

Thank you Caitlin.

She doesn't move. This means she is waiting for me to say something. I hate that. It makes my underarms prickle and get wet. I almost start sucking my sleeve like I do at recess but then I remember. *You're welcome,* I say.

7

She moves away.

I got it right! I go to the refrigerator and put a smiley face sticker on my chart under YOUR MANNERS. Seven more and I get to watch a video.

When I turn away from the fridge I see a puffy blue marshmallow wall in front of me. It smells of apple cinnamon Pop-Tarts and breathes noisily. It's another neighbor or relative. I don't know which. Her hands are shaking. One hand has a tissue and the other hand she holds out to me. There is a white circle in it. *Would you like this candy?*

I don't know. I have never had her candy before so I don't know if I'll like it. But I like just about every candy in the galaxy. I don't like being trapped by the puffy blue wall like this though.

Take it, she says, and pushes it into my hand.

So I take it just to get her hand off of mine because her hand is squishy and flabby and makes me feel sick.

Have another, she says.

I take it quickly so I won't have to feel her hand again.

She tries to pat my head with the candy hand but I duck.

I run and hide behind Dad. And eat the candy. They are

mints. I wish they were gummy worms because that's my favorite but I Deal With It. The good thing is I can't talk when my mouth is full because that's rude so if I keep my mouth full I can be in my own Caitlin world.

When I finish the candy I still don't want to talk so I push my head under Dad's sweater and feel the warmth of his chest as he breathes up and down and I smell his Gillette Cool Wave Antiperspirant and Deodorant. He doesn't even say, *No Caitlin,* and pull me out. He lets me stay there and pats my head through the sweater. If it's through the sweater I don't mind. Otherwise I don't like anyone to touch me. Dad talks to the world outside the sweater and his voice makes a low hummy-vibratey feel. I close my eyes and wish I could stay here forever.

Also from Kathryn Erskine:

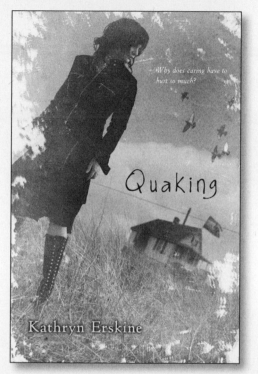

In this compelling young adult novel, goth-girl Matt must find the strength within to help make a difference in herself and in the world.